The Empathetic Brother

Opening Dedication:

This book is dedicated to the love that doesn't always have a conventional beginning. The madness that people find love through, the grief that can lead to new, unexpected beginnings. This book is dedicated to the love that most wouldn't root for, but I do.

Stay strong, unconventional Lovers.

The Empathetic Brother

Written by Kristen Elizabeth

Table of Contents:

Opening Dedication:..2
Table of Contents:..3
The Empathetic Brother Muse Playlist 5
Disclaimer Notice: 7
Author's Warning:...8
Special Author's Note:...9
Kathryn Abraham… 12
Kenneth Jayce-Soren…...23
Kenneth… 43
Kenneth… 58
Kathryn Soren… 67
Kathryn… 79
Killian Jayce… 94
Kathryn…...112
Kathryn…...127
Kathryn…...144
Killian… 152
Killian… 164
Kathryn…...178
Kathryn…...188

Killian…	203
Killian…	215
Kathryn…	226
Killian…	239
Epilogue – Aaron Renaldas	248
Bonus Chapter 1 – Carson Soren…	252
Author's Medical Corner:	256
Extras:	262
Book 9 Excerpt	267
Books by Kristen Elizabeth	275
Acknowledgments	278
About the Author	280
Author Q&A	282
About this Book	284
Reader's Observing Questions:	287
Final Remarks	292

The Empathetic Brother Muse Playlist

(Alphabetical Order)

Book 8 Theme: Bring Me the Horizon - DArkSide

Muse Playlist (Alphabetical Order)

1. 30 Seconds to Mars – From Yesterday
2. American Authors – Luck
3. Anastacia – Take This Chance
4. Billy Squire – Emotions in Motion
5. Billy Squire – Rock me tonight
6. Bon Jovi – Bed of Roses
7. Camila Cabello – Havana
8. Breaking Benjamin – Give me a Sign
9. Breaking Benjamin – The Diary of Janes
10. Bullet for My Valentine – Tears Don't Fall
11. Citizen Soldier – Death of Me
12. Citizen Soldier – Unbreakable
13. Clean Bandit – Rather Be
14. Cody Johnson – 'til You Can't
15. Elise Azkoul – La Vie En Rose
16. Evanescence – Cloud 9
17. Evanescence – Lacrymosa
18. Imminence – Heaven in Hiding
19. In this Moment – Forever

20. Linkin Park – No More Sorrow
21. Motionless In White: Another Life (disguise)
22. KATHRYN THEME: 2CELLOS – We found Love
23. KENNETH THEME: Max-Music – Tension
24. KILLIAN THEME: 2CELLOS – Use Somebody
25. Little mix – Change your Life
26. Paloma Faith – Only Love Can Hurt Like This
27. Seether – Fine Again
28. The Chainsmokers – Roses
29. Three Days Grace – Break
30. Tool – Schism
31. Queen Naija – Butterflies
32. Witchz – Seasons

Disclaimer Notice:

Disclaimer Notice:

All of the art in this novel series is drawn by the author, Kristen Elizabeth.
By no means am I a professional artist, nor do I claim to be, but I've always enjoyed the hobby.
I hope the drawings help you to integrate even further into this novel's world.
Thank you for reading!

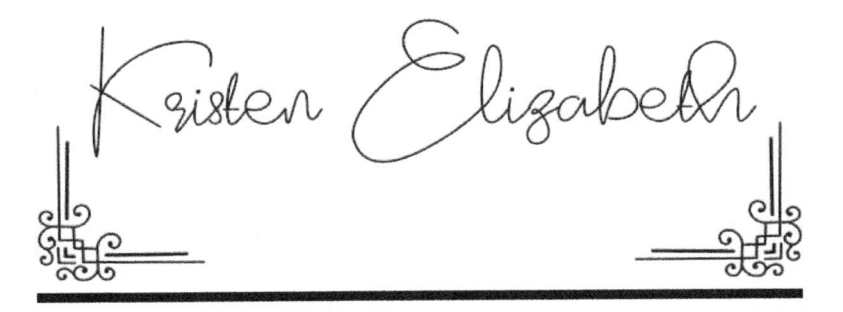

Kristen Elizabeth

Author's Warning:

This book contains trigger warnings and material, including:

Abandonment/Neglect
Bullying
Sexual Assault
Explicit content
Lying/Cheating
Murder/Gore
Abuse

Please proceed with caution, and if triggered by any of these themes or by the story, please seek the appropriate help or resources. Be safe! Thank you!

Special Author's Note:

This novel saga uses an entirely different Calendar system, with different names of the months and days of the week. So, the Months and Weekdays are as follows:

January – Blizzard's Reign (30 days)
February – Nivis's End (20 days)
March – Seed's Sewn (40 days)
April – Rain's Fall (40 days)
May – Veras's Height (40 days)
June – Veras's End (20 days)
July – Solaris's Gifts (30 days)
August – Solaris's Reign (40 days)
September – Solaris's End (20 days)
October – Moon's Dance (27 days)
November – Folias's Blessing (30 days)
December – Year's Fall (20 days)

Sunday – Sun's Dawning
Monday – Morning's Stars
Tuesday – Seed's Rising
Wednesday – Sun's Reign
Thursday – Sun's Falling
Friday – Twilight's Reign
Saturday – Moon's Height

Spring – Veras
Summer – Solaris
Autumn – Folias
Winter – Nivis

Preface

Kathryn Abraham...

Solaris's End, 1314 Imperial Lunar Year

"Well, I have some good news for you, young master Kenneth and Young master Killian!" The butler said as he stepped out of the office where our parents were, a big smile on his face. "As of today, Lady Kathryn is the betrothed of young master Kenneth," the butler informed us, and we all startled.

I looked at the two brothers in front of me, gaping at them.

"W-what?" I asked, stunned. I looked to the butler. "That can't be true!" I cried. I ran up to him, grabbing his arms and shaking him—admittedly, a very un-lady-like reaction... "You must be lying!" I cried. "I'm not even of age! It isn't true!"

"It is, young miss!" He said, cheerful. Why was he so cheerful? I didn't want to get married! Especially not to someone whom I had just met! Why was he so excited? "Your parents are setting up the contract as we speak. I am sure that you will be a great bride for the young master."

"But I...I don't even know him!" I shouted, pointing. "This is the first time we've ever even met! Haven't we moved past this, as a society?!" I cried. "This is unfair!"

"Now, now, miss," the maid tried to hush me. "I know that he is our second young master, so his rank isn't quite as high, but he will still be a fine match! As the daughter of a marquess, it is still an honor to marry someone of the same rank—"

"I don't care about *rank*!" I shouted. "I don't love him! I haven't even had my debut! A young lady is supposed to, to...to have her debut, meet a man among her peers and start going through formal courting! It is supposed to be romantic and whimsical like a dream! An arranged marriage is...it is archaic! Ancient! Outdated!" I cried. "I do not love him, and I truly believe that I *never will*," I huffed, crossing my arms, and turning, stomping my foot. "This is extortion. Absurdity! Our society almost never even does arranged marriages anymore! I should be able to marry who I love, not someone set up through a contract! I won't love someone I'm *forced* to marry!"

"I won't ever love *you*, either, then!" My new fiancé shouted. "Grow up and stop being such a child! What kind of lady acts like this when she hears something she doesn't like? It isn't like arranged marriages *never* happen. It might not be very common anymore, but we're nobles. How about *you* act like it?! It isn't like *I* have a choice, either! You act like you're the only one affected! What, you think *I* would choose a bride like *you*? You may as well be a dog, with the way that you're barking with that mouth, in that deranged fashion!"

I whirled around. "You take that back! I'm not a dog!"

"Bark, bark, *bark*!" He shouted. "That's all you can do! Barking like a mongrel! Woof!"

"Oh, *my*," we heard a new voice from the entryway, and we all glanced at our parents standing there, looking upon the scene with varying expressions.

My father looked on with a sharpy frigid expression that made tingles run down my spine. I knew the look well...I had faced it before.

My mother's face was the opposite of his: boiling over with righteous fury.

I could be expecting the crop on the back of my legs, later.

Their parents looked concerned, and a bit nervous.

"What have we here?" Their father asked. "We heard a commotion. Is everything alright?"

I pointed at the younger of the two brothers. "You aren't really marrying me off to him, are you?" I cried. "An arranged marriage, without my consent?!"

The butler bowed deeply to our parents. "It seems that I made a grave blunder in telling them...I thought that they would be *excited*, as they seemed to be getting along rather well beforehand... I had thought that they understood the meaning behind today's meeting, and I didn't anticipate that the news would bring this kind of upset..."

"Of course, it would!" I shouted. "I haven't even had my social debut! And I'm being sold off to this...this jerk!" I screamed.

My father stormed across the room in my direction, and before I even knew what was happening, he was striking me hard across the face just as the fear was rapidly shooting to the brim of my mind.

Both the brothers both flinched and gaped at the scene, eyes wide.

I looked up at my father, gaping in shock.

He had never been particularly kind.

In fact, he'd always been rather dissociative and hurtful and mean...but he'd never struck me in the *face*. He had never struck me, himself, personally, in any fashion.

That wasn't to say that I wasn't disciplined, however.

I had been whipped on the back of the legs during my tutoring and etiquette lessons, but never had I been stuck in the *face*...

I had also never been struck in front of *other people*, and my cheeks flamed with shame and embarrassment, making the rapidly-forming bruise hurt a lot more.

"This isn't for *you* to decide, and how dare you behave as such. You are the daughter of a marquess. Act like it. *Now.*"

Tears rolled down my face, and as I tried to turn to flee the room, he snatched my arm and practically ripped me backward.

The wind knocked out of me as he pulled me, and I gasped, choking mid-breath. Pain locked in my shoulder as it felt like the tendons tore.

I sputtered and sobbed as he slapped the other cheek just as hard as he had struck the first.

"You dare to act so impudently while *I'm still speaking to you?*" He gaped at me, rage in his eyes. He turned to the Duke of Jayce, bowing. "I am so sorry, Duke Jayce. I will be sure to strip these...these foul, ludicrous *behaviors* from my daughter *thoroughly* before she is wed to your son, so I pray that you can please ignore and forget about this unruly outburst."

The duke waved it off, a somewhat sympathetic look on his face as he glanced over at me with a guilty expression. "It *is* a lot to take in and process. This is, after all, our first-time meeting. Arranged marriages are also uncommon nowadays, and young ladies expect to debut and court a man of mutual interest in one another. Most young ladies don't face an arranged marriage without their consent like this, so I didn't think it would go over perfectly. I can empathize..."

I glanced at the brothers.

The Jayce family was descended from the Ashland family of old, and the features from this ancient family were still able to be seen, even now, in this family.

The older brother was tall, with sleek, shiny, dark brown hair and golden-green eyes. He was handsome, with growing musculature from knight training.

He was the heir to the Jayce duchy, and as such, he had to be a good knight. He looked a lot like his father, who had the same coloring of hair and eyes, and sharp facial features, just like him, and a broad and strong, tall body.

His father may be the duke, but their mother was previously the Marchioness of Soren, who had inherited the title from her father—who, like his daughter, had no siblings.

So, the duke and duchess' second son, Kenneth—who had his mother's tussled, rich, sandy blonde hair and his father's striking golden-green gaze—was going to be the next Marquess of his mother's former title.

I was going to be marrying *him*.

I would be the next Marchioness Soren…

I was the second child of Marquess Abraham, and as he already had a son to inherit his title, he needed me; He needed to marry me off, to make a strong alliance through marriage.

I just hadn't expected to be married off before my own social debut.

I had truly been of the belief that I would have my social debut, meet a well-known, well thought of noble gentleman, and bring honor to—and escape from—my family, in a peaceful and blissful marriage.

It seemed that fate, however, would not be so kind as to grant my childish, whimsical daydream.

"We will schedule for the marriage to take place next month, then," my mother said, and I startled.

"What?" I cried.

Both of the brothers also startled at this information.

"*The Marquess*," their mother whispered. "He has taken ill. He has asked for me to go ahead and have you succeed the title, since I am now the duchess rather than the Marchioness," she told Kenneth, and he gasped.

"Oh," he said, whispering. "I see."

Ah, so that was the rush.

Without an heir to take over the marquess household, and as the only heir was married to the duke...they needed to have the next heir take his place.

If no heir stepped up, the title would pass to the monarchy, and the monarchy could do whatever they wanted with the peerage. As long as an heir stepped up, ready to take the title—or had someone to hold the title for them, until they were of age, as long as they were unmarried and willing—the monarchy couldn't touch the title of that family.

To become the marquess at his age, he would need to marry almost right away to have the extra support and stability from another house to help him secure the title more thoroughly.

That meant that this marriage wasn't *just* an alliance to his *family*, but a desperate move to help him take over his title.

By helping him, my family would be expecting his support in return, when he had more ability to do so after he took well to being the new marquess.

It was a power move, and *I* was the key.

I swallowed this fact bitterly, knowing that I had no say-so in the matter, when I opened my mouth and my father reared back his hand again.

The brothers flinched once more, giving me wearily sympathetic glances.

...I didn't want their pity.

If they pitied me, that just made me feel even more pathetic and sorry.

"We will see you then." Duke Jayce said. "And, the dowry?"

"Secured and prepared for transfer right away," my father said.

I swallowed back bile in my throat.

Dowry...because it was customary for not only the bride's parents to pay for the *wedding*, but to pay an...appreciation fee to a man for choosing their daughter!

They were bribing this family to take me, so to speak.

They liked to claim that it was for a woman to bring to her new home, to live on, and use as her own personal funds and help her settle into her new home...but that usually wasn't the case.

The dowry *usually* went to the man, and he used it however he pleased, claiming that she could just live on the house's funds.

Women were more like auction items, it seemed.

I could see no difference in this case, either.

They may as *well* have been saying, "Hello, thank you for choosing to marry our child. Here is some compensation for taking this unwanted mouth to feed off of our hands. Let's be friends!"

They certainly were going to be well compensated for the burden of taking me on...

"We will seal this agreement with the verbal agreement and kiss seal between them," the duke said.

Fear rattled my body even as my mind went numb and my heart pounded.

Our parents stepped closer together, bringing us with them, and they had us hold hands...albeit with a bit of difficulty.

Upon a glance and nod from the duke, Kenneth glanced at me, before staring at our joined hands, not looking at my face. "I vow to marry this lady, Kathryn Abraham, on the decided upon day. I will honor this arrangement and hold true to it, and I will not dishonor my fiancé by backing out or refusing to marry her. On my honor as the son of Duke Sebastian Jayce."

I was too numbed to really know what was going on, and Kenneth squeezed my hand, clearing his throat as my father nudged me from behind.

"Speak, damn you!" My father grunted at me from behind my back.

"Oh..." I cleared my throat, my voice barely audible. "I vow to marry this man, Lord Kenneth Jayce, on the decided upon day. I will honor this arrangement and hold true to it, and I will not dishonor my fiancé by backing out or refusing to marry him...On my honor as the daughter of Marquess Jacob Abraham."

"A kiss of agreement is necessary, my lords," the lawyer nearby said quietly.

Of course, it was...

When he saw me glance away, Kenneth let out a soft breath, before he leaned forward, pressing his lips softly to my own, chaste and like a whisper, before he pulled away, but he kept his hold on my hands and wouldn't let me jerk mine away as our fathers and the lawyer stepped off to the side to talk.

"Just wait," he whispered. "Unless you want your father to slap you again," he murmured as the men spoke business nearby.

I hated that he seemed to actually be looking out for me, and that I needed to heed his advice.

I hated this whole situation.

Though...it wasn't as if I ever had a choice, to begin with.

There was a reason that I couldn't speak up, though, that even I had no knowledge of at this point in time.

"Alright," Duke Jayce said, bringing the men back over to us. "We will see it done. Please have a safe journey back home."

As my parents went to gather our coats from the butler, Kenneth leaned forward again.

"I am sorry," he whispered. "I promise...it will be alright," he said, giving me a sad smile, soft. "We may not be able to love each other, but I will do my best to not be mean to you. I've seen how your father is, and what kind of life you must have at home...so I will try to be good to you. It will be alright."

I clenched my eyes closed, finally jerking my hands away from him.

How dare he make a promise like that?

Didn't he know that I was just a cow that had been sold off to his family?

I was property, now.

How could everything be alright, when nobody cared about my feelings?

Even if he didn't have any control over this, he could have tried a little harder to not accept it.

He could have pushed back, right?

He was a man, so they would listen to him, wouldn't they?

"No," I whispered, almost choked. "It will never be alright again. I've just been *sold*, like cattle. I didn't even have a chance to meet anyone or be courted, or find love on my own...even who I escape the marquess from in marriage is something that he, as always, gets to choose for me. I have no say in anything in my life... I'm just an *object*," I said, tears running down my cheeks.

I opened my eyes to see his own again, and I cringed at the pained and bothered expression I saw there.

I ignored the burning pit in my belly as I turned, rushing after my parents as we left the estate.

When we returned back to our manor, I was on the receiving end of a severe lashing, as I had expected, while my brother tried desperately to get my father to stop before he severely injured me.

In the end, I spent the rest of the week lying in bed, being neglected by the maids...and the only one I had nursing me was my brother, who had to sneak medicine to me in the middle of the nights.

Otherwise...I was alone.

Chapter 1

Kenneth Jayce-Soren...

Solaris's End, 1314 Imperial Lunar Year

"We have guests coming today?" I asked, surprised. "Who?"

"Marquess Abraham, his wife, and their daughter Kathryn, young master Kenneth."

I felt my stomach drop, suddenly, but I wasn't entirely sure why.

I already knew who the Marquess and his wife were...and that their rarely-spoken-about daughter was of a similar age as myself.

It was peculiar to me, how they were bringing their daughter, whom was almost never mentioned in society.

Why was that...?

The highest probable reason for them to be bringing her was likely a marriage alliance, but that would be unusual in today's times.

Arranged marriages were uncommon, nowadays.

In today's society, a woman would make her social debut into high society, and men would seek to court her.

Whenever she found a man who had mutual interest in her, and their families were of good alignment, they would begin courting and he would propose after a few months, if they had agreed to marry.

I knew that the Marquess had a son, as well; his heir...but if he were coming with just himself, the marchioness, and his *daughter*?

I could see no other reason *other* than a marriage...so...

She would probably end up as my sister-in-law, I figured.

My brother had faced a great number of women expressing interest in marriage with him and courting, but he had turned them all down.

He had to have high standards, as the next Duke of Jayce, as it were.

Our family was particularly important to trade in the empire, and to the imperial family. He could not just choose any bride that he wished.

He had to think about it seriously.

I certainly wouldn't think that she was being brought to be matched with me, but if she was not here to be matched with Killian, then...

I had recently turned sixteen...therefore, I had recently made my debut into high society, and I'd had several marriage requests given to my parents from families already...although none of those families had been approved, and *certainly* none of them had come to visit us at our family home...

Did this mean that this family was "the one" that my family had actually accepted?

I sighed.

I'd heard about Marquess Abraham...he was one of the wealthiest among the nobility.

He had a high standing as a powerful knight and war hero, as well as a powerful prosecutor in the court legal system. He was one of the emperor's favored relatives, and definitely a reliable ally to have.

...He was, however also known to be rigid, strict, and have a vile temper.

I knew that they had a son who was seventeen, and a daughter who was fourteen; still yet to make her debut.

"Did her family put in a request to visit our estate?" My older brother asked.

My older brother, Killian, was seventeen, and it wouldn't be long before he turned eighteen; though he had longer before he was expected to marry, it would still be arranged and settled soon.

He had longer until he got his title, since he was the heir to the duchy rather than the marquess title from our mother.

Our mother was the daughter of a Marquess who was on his deathbed, and as a woman, she couldn't inherit the title, so her son—the second-born, who wasn't receiving his father's title...as in, myself—would be receiving the title from her father.

My elder brother would inherit the duke's title when he turned twenty-one, but I would become the Marquess of Soren before he became the duke.

"Actually, young master...it was *your* parents who reached out to Marquess Abraham first," the butler informed us.

I startled. "*My* parents requested *them*? Whatever for?" I asked.

Perhaps it *wasn't* about marriage, after all. How very odd.

Usually, the family of the lower rank was the one to reach out for a marriage alliance. My father was a duke, and the Marquess was below him.

It was highly unorthodox for a young man's *parents* to reach out to a girl's parents to ask for their daughter's hand in marriage, anyway. Even if the man was higher in rank, if he found a woman he wanted to marry, he could ask her parents himself...

Usually, if a man was interested in a young lady, he would make the request himself. His parents did not get involved unless it was to intervene and stop the marriage for whatever reason, though that almost never happened. It was unheard of.

For arranged marriages, however, the lower ranked families—usually the lady's family—would request the arrangement.

If a man came from a wealthy, high-ranked family, women's parents would often put in bids for the son to seek out their daughter at her debut first, to get in a good chance for a courtship...but it was unheard of for a man's *parents* to reach out to another family to make an arranged marriage this way.

So...what other business could they be here for?

I racked my brain trying to uncover the mystery.

When they had arrived, our parents had left the room to go and speak in the office, leaving the girl to be entertained by my older brother and myself.

Optimistic that her family wasn't here for marriage after all, we had smiled and enjoyed a word game, laughing, and sipping tea, eating sweet treats.

She was admittedly very pretty, with ashy gray-blonde hair and eyes that reminded me of amethyst; almost a purple-blue color. She was a very pretty young lady.

She likely had mage-blood in her, with her colorings. She looked Mage-Born.

Light hair and light eyes were usually mage traits.

It was odd, though, that she had come with her parents alone. I had anticipated to see the entire family, if this were regular business.

Their son would have attended to learn more about business, as well.

It still seemed rather odd...

Her brother, apparently, had stayed at the Abraham estate that day. He was set to inherit the Marquess title when he turned twenty-one, the way that my brother would inherit the duke's title at the same age.

Things had been going so well, and we had been enjoying the visit...

The maids had giggled as they watched my brother and I interacting with her, and the butler had been watching with a big grin on his face...

Of course, I would find out later, however, that marriage was, indeed, the reason behind asking the Abraham family to the estate.

I had anticipated that the marriage would be between her and Killian, but that wasn't the case.

It was me...

I was still in shock.

My parents wanted to discuss the terms of the contractual marriage in person, and explain why they were putting in the request rather than the other way around.

As it had turned out, Kathryn Abraham was the *only* girl around my age who had been available for marriage so *quickly*, who wasn't already being courted or already betrothed.

This was, of course, because she hadn't made her social debut yet, and wasn't out in the marriage market to find a suitor. In fact, nary a word had been spoken about her much in public, and there were even rumors and whispers that she may not get to make her social debut.

Nobody quite knew the reason that the Marquess and Marchioness didn't care to talk about their daughter and brag about her, the way that most noble families would, but it always seemed rather strange.

Now, an arranged marriage out of nowhere, without even considering our opinions?

They truly were taking the choice away from us both...

Generally, if a couple were arranged to be married this way, they would have a trial period of courting before the official announcement of the engagement, just to ensure that the couple could get along and were compatible with one another.

We didn't have the luxury of waiting that long, as the wedding would be taking place in less than three months.

One would think and be under the impression that I'd already had her bedded and pregnant, with the way that we were rushing this wedding.

It was because my grandfather had taken ill for the worst during the night, and wasn't expected to live past the next two months...so, we were scheduled to marry the following month, and I would then inherit the title.

Still, there was the fear of taking this girl I didn't even know as my bride.

I'd flinched and startled when my new fiancé had been struck for being upset, and I was concerned for her upon their exit...that had seemed overly harsh, and what was even worse, were...

The dark promises in the Marquess' words implied that she would be further disciplined when they got home, and I could only hope that she wouldn't blame me or my family for putting her into such a position.

I knew that if it hadn't been for the announcement, she wouldn't have gotten upset.

Moon's Dance, 1314 ILY

I sat, knees apart, elbows on my knees and chin on the back of my clasped hands, nervous as I waited on the ceremony to start.

She had been so...so *hurt*, by the engagement.

There hadn't even been an engagement party, which was a tradition almost all noble ladies could count on.

All except for my bride to be.

She was being excluded out of everything that most noble brides got to look forward to.

I knew that things were happening all out of proper order, and I had to admit that I felt very guilty that she wasn't even getting a *proper* experience. It wasn't fair; not for either of us.

It was one thing to be put into a political or arranged marriage, but to not even have had an engagement party, or a bridal shower...?

To be pushed through to the ceremony in a month's time and be expected to just be okay with it?

No celebration, no excitement...just rushing to get through the even with no fanfare or care?

It was odd, really. Something about it was *suspicious*, almost.

She wasn't even able to express her displeasure without physical reprimand...

I knew that this was no common in our society, not for noble ladies, but...I couldn't put my finger on the reason.

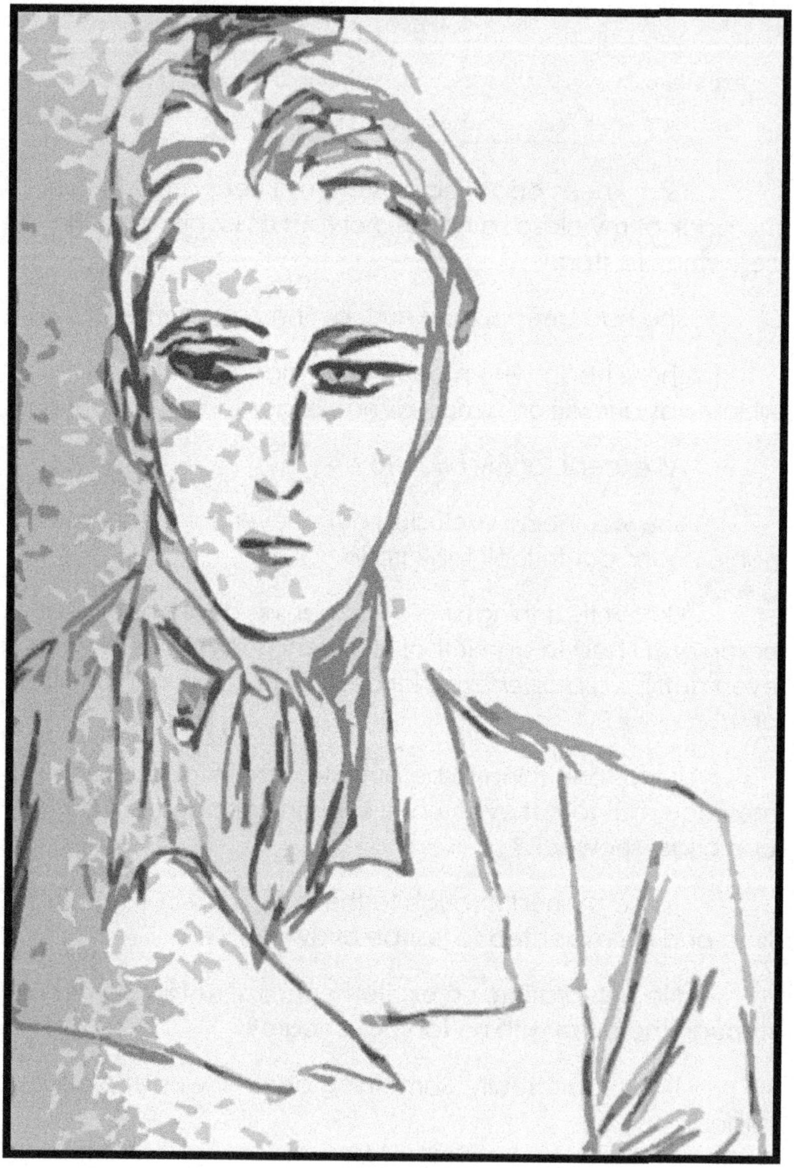

It was very unfair to my young bride.

Typically, a woman would have her social debut and men would cue up to meet her at banquets and parties.

Then, if the woman found a man that she was interested in who had expressed interest in her, then her family would send the request for marriage on behalf of their daughter if the man hadn't already done so himself, and it would be mulled over and considered for about a month before it was accepted or rejected.

Upon acceptance, that would be sent back to the requesting family, and then a date would be agreed upon to meet at a formal engagement party.

The engagement usually lasted close to a year, even two, before the couple were wed. This was to give them plenty of time to get acquainted socially and debut *together* in society, attending parties together to raise their families' statuses.

Then, there would be the bridal shower, where the couple would receive guests and gifts, and their new home would be decided upon for when the nuptials took place.

There would be a bachelorette and bachelor party, and then, finally, the wedding day, before the wedding night.

However, my grandfather was—quite literally—lying on his deathbed, even at this moment.

It was imperative that I marry quickly, and move to my new Marquessate.

I was going to be hyphenating the Jayce name with my mother's maiden Marchioness name: I would be going from Kenneth Robert Jayce, to Marquess Kenneth Robert Jayce-Soren.

My father and brother stepped into the room, giving me a sympathetic look.

"You look good, son," my father said.

I smiled at him, sadly. "Have you seen the bride?"

"Yes...she looks lovely, and nervous...very nervous," Killian said, looking off at the wall awkwardly. "Almost nauseated looking, actually."

"Oh," I murmured.

So, she wasn't doing well...

"I brought you something." My father said, and he reached in his pocket, and pulled out a pocket watch. "Your grandfather gave me a watch when I got married to your mother...He told me that it was imperative to always be on time, and be punctual for my wife...that it would help me a lot in our marriage. And, he was right. It truly has. The giving of a pocket watch has been done for generations. it is a Jayce family tradition."

I hesitated, before I took it. It was a nice pocket watch; very high-quality.

"Thank you, father..."

He scratched the back of his head. "I know that this...wasn't your *ideal* situation. Trust me, I know that for the both of you, you are out of your depth and unhappy. Truly, I understand that you are apprehensive, that you are nervous and undoubtedly frustrated. However, I have known Marquess Abraham for many years. I'd never met his young lady, though I've met his son before. I know that it was...a rough situation when we met her a month ago, due to the sudden news that was dropped onto her lap, but I am sure that she is a nice young lady, as she comes from such a well-respected and *disciplined* family."

Disciplined family, huh?

More like *abusive*...but I didn't say that aloud.

"She was *very* nice before the news came to us," my brother reminded. "She had a good, sweet disposition and enjoyed learning the word games we were playing. She seems nice."

I sighed. "It is just...I feel like this is so unfair to *her*...I know that she isn't getting to experience things the way that a lady normally would."

"I am sure she will adjust—"

"*Most* ladies don't even get married before their debut, even if they are betrothed beforehand—though even *that* is rare. And what of her *debut*? Is she still to have a debut? Now that she will be a married woman, does she still need to have a debut into high society?" I asked, overwhelmed by this newest problem coming to light in my mind. "And if she does, is that left to be my responsibility now? I don't even know how to be a husband...I have only recently begun learning the rules and duties of being a marquess, and now I have to figure out how to be a husband, too? How to be a woman's keeper?"

My father patted my shoulder. "Yes, she will need to be debuted into high society, if she is to have any friends and allies in the high social circles. That is an important aspect of being a noblewoman, but especially a high-ranked lady of a house, like a marchioness. Yes, giving her the social debut will technically fall onto *you*, but the *staff* can do the majority of the planning for it, and I am sure that her parents, or even I, would be willing to help you when the time comes. Being a husband...is rather simple, really, and my greatest advice to you would be this; *patience*."

I sighed. "I understand...but..." I blushed. "What about the...marriage act? Am I expected to have my first night with her *now*? *She's* not even of age yet."

My father looked away. "Well," he hesitated. "It *is* important to seal the marriage with the consummation. That is something that had been agreed upon for the contract, itself, so that is required, unfortunately...lest her parents get the idea that you will just give their daughter *back* after getting their backing to become the next Marquess Soren and you have your funds and backing from them." he told me, and I startled.

"What?" I asked horrified. "G-give...her back? Did you just say that?"

"It will be vitally important to give them proof that you fully take her as your bride, and that you have no intent to return her after receiving their aid."

"Return her...?"

He nodded. "You are, *technically*, able to return her to her parents before the marriage is consummated. Until the marriage is properly consummated, then she isn't your wife in anything but *title*. You have to make her your bride in every way...in the way that a man would make a woman his bride."

I swallowed thickly. "But I've...I haven't even kissed anyone."

"Kissing isn't that big of a deal," my brother said. "I've had my first kiss. I kissed a maid, and it was because I asked her if I could so that I could get it out of the way and my friends would stop picking on me," he laughed.

I groaned, covering my face with my hand, when the butler arrived at the door of my room.

"The ceremony is ready to begin, my lords. It is time to go," he told us.

With final glances at one another, we left the room, going out to the banquet court, having a cool, outdoor Folias wedding.

It was a warm afternoon for Moon's Dance, and everything was decorated for Folias weather.

I went to stand at the end of the aisle with the priest, standing in front of all of our friends and family, when the violinists began to play, cueing the bride.

I glanced up, watching as she and her father slowly emerged from the estate, and I looked upon my bride-to-be as they strode toward me in time with the music.

She looked pretty in her gown; a simple gown with beautiful lace and embroidery in silver thread along the sleeves of her gown.

It was a modest dress, covering her to preserve her honor, rather than an older bride who might show a little skin on her chest to provoke a lustful reaction from the groom.

This wedding, however, was for a bride who had *yet* to even come-of-age and have her social debut.

She had a veil covering her face, and her hair was pulled back into a braided bun, clipped back with sapphire clips.

She was prettily but modestly decorated, my child-like bride.

Only our families were even attending this quickly-put-together wedding.

It was a very private affair, honestly, though the family and staff made sure that everything was pretty, for the sake of the trembling bride.

I was honestly surprised by the lack of attendees for my bride. I had relatives from my families on both sides, my father and mother, who came to support me...but the only guests who came with my bride were her mother, father, and brother.

It was...very odd.

I wondered if that was why she was struggling so much.

Did she truly have such little support at home?

I could see that she was trembling, even as she tried so hard to hold her reserved expression and demeanor.

It was obvious after her outburst when she'd gotten the news to begin with, she'd faced severe scolding and was determined to behave as she was expected for this unequivocally, momentously important event in our families. I could tell, quite easily, that it was a regular disciplinary action that she faced, and she knew well enough that if she didn't behave as expected, she could absolutely expect that physical reprimand.

It was heartbreaking to see the way she trembled and held herself with such fear.

Finally, they reached the alter and I took her hand from her father's.

"Welcome, family and friends, to the union of the houses Jayce, Soren and Abraham!" The priest announced. "In the sight of God and kin, we gather here today to watch this young couple enter into a holy contract, of mutual benefit and understanding. Kenneth Jayce-Soren, you are so named the Marquess of Soren from henceforth with this marriage, and are expected to perform your duties honorably and dutifully. Do you, Kenneth Jayce-Soren, take Kathryn Abraham to be your lawfully wedded wife? Do you promise to honor her, care for her, and perform your duties toward her?"

I swallowed thickly. "I do," I said.

"Do you, Kathryn Abraham, take Kenneth Jayce-Soren, to be your lawfully wedded husband? Do you promise to honor him, care for him, and perform your duties toward him?" The priest asked.

I saw the hesitations there, felt the tension in the air, but her father cleared his throat quietly and she flinched.

"I-I do," she muttered out softly.

"By the authority invested in me by the church of God and by the king of our country, I name you husband and wife. You may now kiss your bride!" The priest declared.

I reached up, careful to control the shaking in my hands, and lifted the veil from her face, laying it back on her head, before I leaned forward, pressing a chaste kiss to her cool lips, before I got a good look at her face.

Her eyes were rimmed-red, red, and puffy from crying, and her cheeks were slightly puffy as well, despite the generously applied makeup that was used in an effort to hide it.

Her eyes darted to the crowed, cheeks flushing with embarrassment.

She didn't want anyone to see how distraught she was, as it was unbecoming of a bride to look as such on her wedding day.

She gave me a defeated expression, one of sorrow and shame, and I carefully lifted her veil to replace it over her face again.

She gasped softly, looking at me in surprise, and I leaned in to her again.

"I know you don't want anyone to see you like this," I whispered.

She gave a small nod, before I took her hand in mine and led her up the aisle, leading her to get changed into a more comfortable set of clothes in a spare room while I waited outside the room, before we then set to go back outside to go to the banquet that had been prepared.

We sat and ate—well, I did, in any case...my bride didn't touch a thing—and though many people congratulated me, I couldn't help but throw concerned glances at my bride.

She had changed into a simple gown, and wore a small white hat with a white-netted veil covering the top portion of her face in an attempt to hide her emotional condition.

I knew that she was having a hard time with this.

I dreaded the idea of having to take this girl to her new home only to let the servants wait outside the door waiting for the *"proof"* that I'd successfully completed my *husbandly duties* with her.

I almost shuddered at the thought.

Not that she was unattractive.

She was a *beautiful* girl, even in such an awful state, but I knew that she didn't want this.

She didn't want me.

She would be completely unwilling the entire time, and it was a blow to my honor to have to force such a thing on someone who I knew didn't want that with me.

How was I supposed to proceed?

After eating, toasts and gifts were given to commemorate our union, before she and I loaded up into a car and began our journey to the Marquess Soren estate.

It was a bitterly awkward silence in the car, riding along to the estate.

My poor young bride, two years my junior but feeling much younger in that moment, didn't even look out of the window but rather at her clasped, trembling hands.

She threw wary glances at my lap occasionally, and I felt that there was no doubt that she knew what was about to take place.

I assumed that her parents must have told her that this would be happening, at least, even if they didn't go into detail about the mechanics of it.

Once I had come of age, my tutor had begun teaching me about the mechanics of the bedroom, about how babies came to be made and brought into the world...though, hearing about the general concept and going through it was an entirely separate issue.

I had seen dogs in the midst of copulation, once, but I knew that humans and dogs were different.

After about two hours of riding, we finally arrived to the Soren estate.

I stepped out of the car, and held my hand out for her to take to help her down.

She took it hesitantly, but she was so short that she couldn't actually step out of the car properly and safely without needing to jump down, so I asked for her to excuse me before I wrapped an arm quickly around her waist, lifting her and setting her on her feet.

Then, I took her by the hand and led her to the steps leading up to the estate.

We were almost there...

A young man stood there, waiting for us. He looked to be in his early twenties, with sleeked-back brown hair and blue eyes. He was tall, with a decent physique. He was, quite obviously, in peak physical condition.

Well-built and thick, muscular.

I noted that he had a dagger strapped to his belt, and I remembered that my grandfather's butler had actually saved his life in the past.

He'd had some training, as I could recall.

"Welcome, young Marquess and Marchioness Soren," the new butler greeted me. "My name is Aaron Renaldas, and I am the head butler for this estate. Please do not hesitate to inform me right away if there is anything at all that you need to be taken care of or seen to. I am at your service. It is an honor to welcome the newlywed couple," he said, bowing and gesturing his arm out toward the estate.

"Thank you, Aaron. I would like a light snack and tea, as well as a bath, prepared for the marchioness right away. We've had a long ride, and I am sure she would like to rest a moment. She will also need a personal maid to see to her needs," I told him.

"I have several maids prepared for her already, and I will see to it that all of that is prepared right away, my lord," he said.

He led us up the stairs and into the estate even as all of the other maids and servants went back inside from welcoming us, before Kathryn was led by a maid to what would be her chambers on the opposite side of the manor as mine.

For the time that I waited, I actually followed the butler around.

"Where is grandfather?" I asked. "I had expected to be taken to him first thing."

"Ah, yes, my lord. The Marquess has been quite ill, and so he has been moved to your parent's estate while you and the marchioness were journeying here," he informed me. "Your parents wanted for your bride to feel more at ease here, since she must be rather nervous. I doubt that having an ailing older man here would be a comfort to her."

I hesitated, clearing my throat. "Aaron," I said softly.

He seemed to hear the unease and discomfort in my tone, because he stepped walking, and he gave me his undivided attention. "Have you...*been* with a woman, before?" I asked, blushing.

He smiled. "Yes, my lord. Might I ask why you inquire?"

"Well," I said, blushing harder. "I know the *general* mechanics...that the man's privates enter into the woman's...but I...well, how does one go about pleasuring *her*? Surely it isn't as simple as just removing my trousers and her gown and sticking myself into her, right? My bride is so young, and she is already very upset. I want to make sure she is as pleased as possible."

He blushed. "Oh, *heavens no*, my lord, that would be horrible and possibly physically damaging to the young lady," he smiled. "If I may," he said, grabbing a nearby piece of parchment and a pen before he dipped it in ink and drew out a feminine-shaped body. He circled several areas on the body. "It is a good idea to touch these areas of the female body, my lord. It will bring her to a much higher state of enjoyment. If you strongly focus your...*ahem, oral attentions here*," he said, circling the breasts and the womanhood areas. "Then you will quite fervently prepare her for the insertion. A woman's *first* time is usually tense, so it is *imperative* that you thoroughly prepare her body beforehand, so that she will recover and enjoy it."

"I see," I said, taking mental notes and studying the drawing again closely, eager to learn this quickly and efficiently, for my young bride's sake.

"If I may be bold enough to interject another quick piece of advice, my lord, I *implore* you to wait a moment after you enter her before moving. It will take a moment for her to adjust to the sensation and if you begin moving before she is ready, it could possibly hurt her worse and could cause her to become dry and irritated on the inside."

"You...seem quite thoroughly *knowledgeable* about this," I told him.

He laughed good-naturedly. "I was a personal escort for a young married noblewoman before I became the butler of this estate," he told me. "Her husband had many mistresses and left his poor young wife alone, and so she sought out *my* attentions regularly. At first, she complained that I was unskilled and surly about the ordeal, but I sought out several prostitutes to learn how to please a woman properly because my pride was so hurt. When I next had relations with my mistress, she was quite satisfied, and I continued to improve."

"Wow," I breathed out, fascinated by the story...I was about to ask another question, before a maid stepped into the sitting room with us, giving a curtsy.

Chapter 2

Kenneth...

"She is bathed and waiting for you in your chambers, my lord," she told me, and my heart thumped wildly in my chest, suddenly nervous beyond belief.

My bride was waiting for me in the bridal chamber...

I took a deep breath, and with a wish of good luck from the butler, I climbed the stairs to the second floor of the estate and found my way through the halls, following the maid, to the master suite.

I had my own chambers in the West Wing of the manor, and my bride's chambers were in the East Wing of the manor. The main master bedchambers, however—the bridal chambers—were in the center of the estate.

Two maids waited outside of the door once I stepped inside, and I glanced around the room, taking it in before I spotted her.

She sat in a white robe on the edge of the bed, facing away from me and stroking her still slightly-damp hair nervously.

I swallowed, stepping over to the bed and sitting down beside of her.

She flinched; her gaze fixed to the floor.

I reached out softly, letting my fingers graze her jaw, pushing her hair out of the way.

Her eyes flew to meet mine, almost startling me.

"I know that you...I know that this marriage wasn't *your* choice," I said softly. "I know that you're struggling with all of this. I know that you aren't happy. The reality, however, is that I am your husband, now...and I'm not left with much choice in this matter either, my marchioness. If you would...please be so kind as to cooperate with me, and I will do my utmost to make it as *pleasant* as I can."

She looked away, before glancing at me again, giving a small nod, relenting her permission to me.

I let my fingers stray to the nape of her neck, stroking there softly, and let my other hand come up to cup her cheek, before I leaned in, pressing a kiss to her lips.

She turned stiff, almost unfeeling, and unrelenting, and began to try to push me away when I tried to deepen our contact.

"W-what are you doing?" She asked, alarmed. "Is that necessary?"

I paused. "You..." I sighed. "I thought that, with what we are about to do, you might want for me to give you some intimacy. I was told that I needed to do all of this, to properly prepare your body for...for *that*," I told her.

"For...what? What...what are we about to do? I don't know what you're referring to," she said, and she flinched and closed her eyes.

I froze...for multiple reasons.

That reaction, first of all, meant that she had expected me to strike her. That meant that she, in her former home, would have been struck for asking such an innocent inquiry. Furthermore, she wasn't...aware? She didn't know what I was talking about...?

"...What?" I asked, stunned but finally finding my voice. "Surely, I misheard you..."

"...Prepare my body for what?"

I gaped. "You mean...nobody *told* you?"

She glanced around the room. "I was told that I would only need to wait on your bed in your room, and that *you* would know what to do, and then I would be left alone until I had to give you an heir. I was told to stay still and quiet and not bother you when you're doing what you have to do."

I stared at her, mouth open and eyes wide, for a long moment.

Was she serious?

"What on earth...?" I asked. "I would have thought they would tell you at least the mechanics of what was going to happen!" I put my face in my hands, incredulous. "I cannot believe they sent you so very *unprepared*..."

"I...I'm sorry," she whispered, her voice meek and small. Fragile.

"No, no, please," I said, desperate to soothe her. "Please, Kathryn. it isn't *your* fault. Don't apologize. I just hadn't been expecting for you to be so unaware. Please, ask me any questions you may have. Tell me anything that you feel. I...I won't strike you."

She perked up. "You...you mean it...?"

"Yes," I said, firm. "I will not strike you."

"Alright...well, I will. So...please pardon me, my lord marquess, but...what is *it*? What do you have to do? What is it that we have to do...?" She asked, hugging herself tightly. "Is that...is that why you kissed me?"

I hesitated, looking away. "Yes. I will warn you; we need to take our clothes off, and you will understand why soon enough. I have to use my..." I groaned. "I'll just show you, because as you just said—it is something that I *have* to do. We don't have a choice. *Neither* of us have a choice here, alright? I don't want to do this either, so can you just cooperate with me and not fight me?"

She deliberated. "Just...don't do anything that *isn't* necessary," she said.

"Isn't necessary...?"

She nodded. "I don't know what kissing me has to do with something you have to do, but I'll try not to fight you if it is something that you have no choice in either."

I sighed, feeling the weight taken off if only slightly by her verbally expressed permission, before I kissed her again, pulling her closer and letting my hands roam over her arms and neck.

She cringed and tried to pull away as I began to untie her nightgown, startled and crying out as I pulled it off of her body and she scooted her body quickly up to the headboard of the bed, clinging to the headboard and trembling, nude.

"What..." She sobbed.

"We have to undress, remember? It is required. Please, just trust me."

"But—"

Without a word, I approached her, gripping her wrists in my hands.

It seemed that her body *naturally* fought this, and I would have to be a little firmer about this to get it done.

I pinned her hands above her head with one hand, my other hand jerking her by the leg to pull her to lie down as I got over-top of her.

I kissed my way down her chest, trying to pay attention to the areas that had been shown on the diagram, but she made it exceedingly difficult for me.

Her body thrashed as tears rolled down her face, pulling and tugging away.

"Why are you doing *this*?" She asked. "Is this really what you *have* to do?"

Rage boiled in me at the blatant disregard to education in these matters that her parents had shown, in that moment. No anger directed at her, because her reaction was only normal. It was even expected...

This poor girl was embarrassed, afraid, and completely and inconceivably **horrified**.

In our society, it was considered crass and mannerless for a man to even touch a lady's bare skin without gloves on. Even holding hands without gloves was a highly intimate action in our society.

For her entire body to be being touched with direct bare skin from a man, well...it was extremely shameful, in her mind, due to the lack of proper *education* in this matter.

She hadn't been taught anything about bedroom behaviors...

"Please!" She cried, she said, cheeks flaming red as kiss marks began to swell and darken on her flesh from my attentions.

I flinched at her shrill cry when I slipped my fingers between her legs, feeling the slit there to see that it was, indeed, at least *somewhat* moist.

Despite her alarmed fear and fighting, her body was at least having a mild physiological response to my attentions, and that was at least something. Her breath began to quicken, gasping into the air of the room, panicked.

I let go of her hand for just an instant to try to grab the lubricant oil nearby that I had, thankfully, been advised to prepare beforehand, and her hand clacked against my cheek as she slapped me.

I startled out of my growing lust, frozen in place, as I gaped at her.

I crawled up her body, forcing my way between her legs, and used both hands to pin her hands down, meeting her gaze.

"I was only trying to properly prepare your body for what I'm about to have to do. *Yes*, it was *all* directly related to what we are both being *forced* to do. You think you're the only one being forced?" I asked, rage burning in me. "Sit still and let me get it *over* with already, please!"

"But—"

"You said you would try not to fight me, but you've fought the entire time! I'm trying to make sure you aren't hurt!"

"You didn't tell me it was necessary! I asked!" She sobbed. "I've *been* asking! You didn't hear me!"

"I thought you were *intelligent* enough to understand, *without* me having to vocally respond each and every single time! I was only busy trying to make sure it was a more pleasant experience on *your* behalf!" I shouted, and she flinched beneath me, trembling. I calmed down my tone, lowering my volume. "You asked me not to do anything unnecessary. I was only doing what I needed to in order to make sure it doesn't *hurt* you as bad. Now, hold still and at least try to relax, or this really *will* hurt you. I was trying to rely on your natural lubrication, but you've almost entirely ensured that you have none there. I have to use lubrication oil to make sure that I don't hurt you."

"H-*hurt* me?" She asked, voice small and body still tensed.

There was little else that I could do at this point. I would just have to proceed.

I used my hand to apply the oil to her nether regions before I quickly made myself imagine a woman beneath me who was beautiful, writhing, and heated due to my attentions, *willingly* accepting me, in order to get myself hard enough to perform…

It took a moment, but I finally got my dick hard enough to get inside of her and do its job.

Then, I slipped between the folds and forced my way past the slight barrier holding in place there.

She shrieked, throwing her head back and sobbing.

"It *hurts*!" She cried, gripping to me tightly as she sobbed. "Why does it hurt? You said all that stuff was to make sure it didn't hurt! You lied!"

"It was, I assure you. If I hadn't done all of that, and if I hadn't lubricated you myself, you would have been in a lot *more* pain than this. That will be the last of the pain, I promise," I told her.

I held still, waiting, surprised at how amazing it felt to be inside of her this way.

I'd never been intimate with a woman, not even having had my first kiss before Kathryn. It was warm and moist, almost like a warm, moist, heated velvet blanket enveloping my most sensitive of places.

It felt amazing, and it took *all* of my willpower to hold still even for a few moments.

Finally, her breath stopped being so rapid, and I could feel her easing a bit.

She was finally calming down.

Slowly, I pulled out, before I slid back in easily, and she flinched, startled beneath me.

A pattern developed, and as I continued my attentions, she slowly began to relax and her breathing changed slightly.

This might not be so bad. She seemed to start getting into it a bit more…though her face was still extremely flushed, and she wouldn't look at me.

It was a subtle difference, but it went from a panicked and alarmed breathing pattern with whimpers of pain to a heated, rhythmic, moaning breathing pattern.

She was, slowly, *finally* starting to enjoy the feeling.

I let go of her hands, and she slowly slid her hands up to grasp at my shoulders, holding on as I picked up my pace a bit.

I flinched and groaned as I felt her fingernails dig and drag on the flesh of my back, stinging, but I hardly cared, so lost I was in the blissful pulling and sucking of her womanhood on my body. I reached a hand between us, stimulating between the folds until I felt a "bead" there, and I rolled it slowly with my thumb, soft but steady and firm.

I could feel her getting even tighter still as her breath began to hitch and her eyes closed tightly. She turned her head to the side, gasping and letting her cries rise in pitch.

"Wh-what's happening?" She asked, alarmed. "I-I'm going to break! I will break, please, stop it! I f-feel weird!"

Suddenly, her back bowed and her body thrashed, writing as her nails bit into my skin again, shouting and sobbing out into my chest, biting my shoulder hard enough to draw blood.

I let myself go, in that moment, and she groaned as I throbbed and pumped out seed into her waiting body.

Finally, I thought as I sighed, taking deep recovering breaths as I let my body slide off to rest beside of her own, even as she clutched a folded blanket next to the bed and stood on shaking legs.

"Is...is it done?" She asked. "Did you finish...? Are we done with the required business?"

"I did," I informed her. "We are."

"W-where is my room?" She asked, her voice trembling. "Please...I want to be left alone, now. May I please be left alone, my lord?"

I sighed, standing, and she flinched, stumbling further away from me to the corner of the room, as far away from me as she could get.

Despite having gotten to enjoy it mildly at the end, her reaction still hurt a bit.

I took the sheets from the bed, and I strode unabashedly naked to the door of my room, swinging the doors open and handing the sheets to one maid, before I turned to the other.

"Take the marchioness to her prepared chambers," I said, suddenly feeling beyond weary. "She needs rest."

"Of course, my lord," they both said, and one scurried off with the sheets to deliver to our parents even as the other maid rushed into the room, wrapping my marchioness in her arms, and walking with her, supporting her body as she stumbled here and there with blood trickling down her inner thighs, and I flinched as she was led out and to her chambers on the other side of the estate.

When they were gone, I stepped back into my room, letting myself fall back onto the bed and fall into a light, listless sleep.

The next morning arrived, and I awoke to the curtains being opened and a pot of tea being brewed next to my bedside.

"Good morning, my lord," Aaron smiled, giving a bow. "I hope you had a pleasant evening," he said.

I hesitated. "It wasn't."

He looked sympathetic. "So, the maids were right, then?"

"The maids?" I asked, alarmed. "...Are there rumors already?" I asked, fearing the worst.

I had been worried that my first night with my bride had likely become a spectacle to the staff here in the marquessate.

"Well, my lord, there *is* a rumor going around the mansion that the young marchioness stayed up late into the night, crying and unwilling to even receive any servants."

I sighed. "Yes, that tracks," I said, rubbing my temples. "Is she sleeping now?"

"Yes, my lord," he answered.

I groaned, gripping my hair with my fingers. "It didn't go over well. It didn't go well at all, Aaron. I feel horrible. I had thought by the end that it was getting better, but..."

"I am more than happy to listen if you like, marquess."

"Her parents, her nanny, the maids...*nobody* informed her of anything to do with *anything* intimate. She was so distraught and alarmed just by my *kissing* her. She was horrified when I started touching her. I tried to explain that I wanted to prepare her body, to make sure that she was in as little pain as possible...and she admittedly had no idea what that phrase even *meant*." I rolled my eyes. "She had no idea what was happening." I scoffed, throwing up my hands. "Do these noble houses think that they're doing their daughters a favor by *not* educating them? Do you want to know what *she* was told?"

"What *was* she told, my lord?" He asked, just as baffled as me.

"She was told that all she had to do was sit on my bed in my room and that *I* would know what to do, and then she would be *left alone* until she had to give me an heir! That she just needed to *stay still* and I would take care of everything myself! *In conclusion, they didn't teach her anything!*"

"What?" He asked, aghast. "She must have been so frightened...Noblewomen are raised to believe it is improper to even touch bare skin! How on earth must she have felt, suddenly being touched that way? Someone should have taught her properly..."

"She was *petrified*," I admitted.

"I am so sorry," he said. "You must feel awful."

"I do," I emphasized. "I truly felt like I was raping her the entire time. Aaron, she begged me to stop, asking me if *each and every* action was really necessary."

"Oh, that poor girl…"

"It was so hard to even keep myself aroused long enough to get the job finished."

"…Did…she ever…get to enjoy it, at all?" He asked, nervous sounding. "Please, pardon me if I've overstepped—"

"No, no, it is alright." I sighed. "She finally began to enjoy it after a while, minimally…I had thought that everything would be okay, by that point, because she started to get more into it and enjoy the feeling, and I…" I cleared my throat. "I even made her cum. I thought that would at least make her not so upset, but…but when we finished…She immediately asked to go to her room and ran to the corner, getting as far away from me as possible."

"I see…" He said, sympathetic. "I am sorry, my lord. I am sure she will come around. Just…give her space. Give her plenty of space, and don't pressure her. I am sure if you leave her be, she will come around. I'll talk to her myself, too. Just give her time."

"Time," I sighed. "How long *do* I have until I *need* to have an heir?" I asked.

"Well," he hesitated. "The law tries to insist that nobility have an heir at least on the way within the first year of receiving a title, but since she is still underage, they will end up telling you that you can wait until after her social debut."

"That gives me a little less than two years, then," I said. "She will turn sixteen in Moon's Dance of 1316, and her debut will take place then."

"Yes, my lord."

I sighed, letting my face fall into my hands in despair.

I didn't know what to do. Everything had gone pear shaped. Nothing was right.

"I don't know if I can do this to her again, Aaron. I really, really don't know. I am not sure I could bring myself to touch her again, in an intimate way. Would she even let me? She fought me so hard, Aaron," I sobbed. "I...I actually had to rape my wife for our consummation. I...I feel *dirty*; so, so dirty." I said. "How can I ever hope to earn her forgiveness?"

"I would remind you, my lord, that you weren't exactly given a choice yourself, Marquess," he reminded me gently. "I am sure she will come to understand that soon, if she doesn't already."

"Were the sheets safely delivered?" I asked, rubbing my temples.

"They were, my lord. Your father-in-law sent over the dowry and a declaration of support document in return. Everything is in proper order and was carried out the way that it should be."

I let out a breath of relief and I nodded, standing, and moving to the window, gazing down at my estate. "At least *that* is taken care of, then, and it wasn't in vain. If that hadn't been a requirement, I wouldn't have done it in the first place." Then, I turned to Aaron. "Be sure that she is served the best foods for breakfast, and give her whatever she wants. She deserves it all."

"Will you go to her, my lord?"

I shook my head. "You are right. I need...to give her space, and time. Honestly, I am probably the last person who should be in her sight for a while. She is better off not running into me." I shrugged. "I will forego breakfast this morning. I don't have an appetite. At least, not for food." I sighed. "Oh, to have a bride so pretty but so terrified of me. How I wish that she could want me, and not fear me."

"My lord?"

"It is a terrible thing, to be a man and to crave closeness to a girl who wishes nothing to do with me and was forced into this relationship against her will, though I know that it is only my own body pushing my craving for her."

"...Pardon me, my lord, but I had heard that you weren't actually very fond of her...according to rumors among the staff between the estates, at least...?"

I laughed. "I hadn't been...At first, when I met her, she seemed nice. I was anxious and wary, knowing that a marriage was a possibility but hoping that it wasn't the case. I enjoyed her company, but as soon as it was announced that we were betrothed to one another, and she swore she could never love me...I've been so bitter."

"I can understand how terrible that must have felt."

"But then," I scoffed. "I watched her father strike her, and I saw how she reacted at the wedding today around her father...I realized that she has likely been intimidated and terrified of her father since birth, more than likely, and I realized that she was just a young girl who was forced into a marriage she hadn't wanted. An arranged marriage, when she should have been able to fall in love organically. I feel like a robber."

He nodded, a sympathetic look on his face. "I see."

"Honestly, I feel like I'm losing my senses. I hadn't expected the first night to affect me this way, even despite what a horror show it turned out to be...I got a lot more attached than I had expected, being that she was the person that I had my first taste of intimacy with. My body wants more of her, but my mind is terrified of feeling anything of that nature for her, given the circumstances..." I sighed. "Please, give me the room. I am ready to be alone."

He hesitated, giving me a somber expression, before he turned, leaving the room, leaving me in my tortured reverie.

I knew that I was going to leave her be, and let her stay to herself.

My body wanted and craved her, but I had more control than that.

She didn't want anything to do with me, so I would leave her alone.

I didn't really want to be in this position, either.

Chapter 3

Kenneth...

Year's Fall, 1314 Imperial Lunar Year

It was just going into Year's Fall, just over a month after the wedding.

I had received reports that my young bride hadn't even left her room in the time that we had been living here, and that she also hadn't had any visitors from her former home, either.

That, honestly, had surprised me more than her unwillingness to leave her chambers.

It wasn't unusual for a family to visit their child once they had married and moved to a new home, so...*where were they?*

Frankly, I had to wonder about the state of her relationship with them in the first place, because aside from not visiting...

Her family hadn't even sent a single *letter* to ask about how she was doing.

Did they truly not care?

They certainly didn't seem to. I would have even expected some unannounced visits, at this point...but *nothing?*

My parents visited and sent letters aplenty. I couldn't understand why her family wasn't doing the same.

Pain tugged at my heart to think about how lonely it must be, to realize that your family cares for you so little.

She had just been married off to benefit their family, but they hadn't even bothered to check in on her since she had left.

I wondered about how her life must have been, living in that place. It was obvious, how she must have been treated.

I knew that her father had been quite strict, but I hadn't thought that she would have been regularly abused or neglected there.

She was a high-ranked nobleman's daughter, after all.

Perhaps, one day, when she came to terms and it came time to have a family, she would be happy with a family that she could have a hand in creating herself.

Then, she would be able to feel more at home.

It was that line of thinking that I had been dwelling upon on the early morning that the butler came rushing to my office with the physician, just six weeks after the arrival of my bride and myself to this place.

"My lord! Marquess, we have news for you," butler Aaron said, giving a bow before he turned to the doctor. I gave them my attention, waiting.

"It seems the young madam is with child, my lord," the doctor said.

He smiled; a smile far too bright for this situation.

"...*With child*?" I asked, crossing my arms, and looking away, to the far wall.

"She has missed her cycle and is exhibiting the signs of morning sickness and extreme fatigue, marquess." Despite describing such sickly-sounding state of being, he seemed pleased to announce this to me, and it left a bitter feeling in my gut to hear him describe my bride's pain in such a flippant way. "You both must be quite happy with this development!"

I gaped at him, my pen falling out of my hand. "*Excuse* me?"

"Congratulations, my lord, the marchioness is expecting!" He repeated. "She was quite overwhelmed by this news herself, my lord, but I am sure she must be brimming with joy—"

"You should stop uttering your *nonsense*," I said, one hand up to stop him and the other pressing to my forehead. "I am *sure* that I have heard you incorrectly. How could the marchioness be pregnant? We only had our first night...I have not even *seen*—let alone *touched*—her since then."

He hesitated so long that I wondered if he had heard me at all. Then, however, he acted as if I hadn't even spoken, ignoring what I had said. "Oh, my lord, it only takes *one time* of giving her your seed to cause pregnancy. It may not happen *every* time that you do so, my lord, but it *can* happen at any time that you do so! I am sure you exaggerate, out of modesty! Yes, I am sure you are embarrassed about your intimate affairs, but yes, it only takes a single time!"

I froze.

Pregnant. Kathryn was...pregnant.

A fourteen-year-old girl, freshly married, was now with child.

I felt **sick**.

"You said that she was...overwhelmed...?"

"Oh, yes, my lord, but I am sure that she must be happy—"

"You are a fool," I laughed, feeling almost manic. "There is no *way* that such news would please *my* marchioness, who was forced to marry me against her will and who literally hasn't left her room since she arrived here. You seem to take it as a joke, doctor, but my bride...is not really a bride, and I am not much of a husband. She is only here under force. We had our required consummation...and that was all."

He flinched; eyes wide. "Is...this *not* good news, then, my lord?" He asked, seeming to finally understand the conundrum.

I sighed, not answering him. "You may go," I told him, waving them out, before I turned to Aaron. "I will go and see her," I told him. "It has been a month and a half since I've even laid eyes upon her. Surely, she won't be too...upset, to simply *see me*. Right?"

He hesitated, but he gave a bow and helped me get changed into a more appropriate attire before he led me to the other side of the estate from my side, to where her chambers resided.

I was still saddened to know that despite giving her chambers so far away from my own, she hadn't even stepped foot outside of her bedroom.

I didn't even venture to this side of the estate in order to give her plenty of room. Why could she not understand?

I'd even instructed the maids to make sure she was aware of this.

Still, she hadn't left her rooms. Still, she had chosen to lock herself away.

She had been that afraid to run into me.

I would, however, continue to try to give concessions and considerations for her.

I was responsible for her, now...and now, our child.

A *child*...it was still hard to wrap my head around.

After a soft knock on her door, I stepped inside to find her gazing out of the terrace doors, watching the snow fall with a soft expression on her young face.

"Hello, Kathryn," I spoke softly. She flinched slightly, before she turned to me.

She stood, giving a curtsy respectfully, eyes upon the floor. "My marquess," she said, voice barely audible. "...You look well."

I was surprised that she had spoken to me at all. I hadn't expected that.

She also seemed much calmer than I had expected. A bit too calm, almost.

"I am," I said, cautious. "Are...are you well?"

She smiled softly, without feeling. "I am well, my lord, thank you for your concern."

"I have been worried after you, though I felt that I should give you plenty of space so that I do not upset you. I am happy to see you seem well."

"I appreciate your consideration, my lord. I take it that you have heard the good tidings?"

"I have heard," I said. "Does...does this news upset you? It is alright to be honest with me about your feelings, I am sure that it must be a lot to take in so suddenly."

She simply gave another deep curtsy. "I am well pleased to be able to serve the marquess so quickly. It is an honor to bring you an heir so soon, and it is also a great relief to me. You must be excited."

She was overly formal with me, and I didn't like it.

Why was she acting this way?

I *had* heard from the butler that the maids had mentioned scars upon her calves, and I knew where she had gotten them; they had been struck upon her when she had reacted so unfavorably to the news of our engagement, and they had taken her home and disciplined her.

I'd also heard of older, much older lash scars upon the backs of her thighs and legs, as well as on her rear end. It told tales of harsh and rigorous discipline during her etiquette and ladies' studies growing up.

An old and rarely-implemented measure for teaching children quickly and absolutely.

It was fought against by activists, now, so it may even become illegal, soon enough.

I hadn't noticed any scars on her body myself, personally, on the night that we'd had our intimacy. It had been so difficult to think about anything other than trying to complete the copulation to begin with that I hadn't noticed the marks.

It seemed that she was afraid to be lashed again if she was not so overtly formal with me, however, and she was overly cautious in her manner and attention to be proper.

"You may rest at ease, marchioness. I didn't come here to be treated as a slave master."

"Of course, my lord," she smiled, before she sat down again with that given expression of permission.

"Please, feel no need to be so formal with me in our own home. You will not be scolded if you aren't formal. You are the marchioness in this house, my lady."

She hesitated, glancing at the maids, and I immediately understood the underlying tension in her tensed body at the mention of her rank.

"Butler Aaron," I said, and he bowed, ready and waiting. "Has the marchioness been amongst the maids' gossip and bullying?"

The maids flinched, falling to their knees, and bowing at my feet as the butler confirmed this for me quickly...as if their own reactions hadn't been confirmations.

"What has this gossip entailed?" I asked.

As the information was revealed to me, and I heard that the maids had been gossiping about what a fake noblewoman my wife was.

How a *proper* noblewoman would serve her husband and treat him with respect, how she hadn't been taught proper manners and she wouldn't be here very long before I expelled her from the manor...

I was enraged by this gossip.

There were even rumors about my wife being an illegitimate child, for heaven's sakes! That could seriously damage her reputation.

"So, you have taken it upon yourselves to scold my bride for being displeased with her situation? To tell her that I would kick her out and send her home if she didn't treat me as a god?" I asked, and they trembled as they pleaded for mercy.

"My-my lord..." Kathryn stopped me, placing her hand on my forearm. "They were right. It isn't their faults. Please, do not be so harsh to them. They have taken good care of me."

"*Good care?*" I asked, startled, and horrified. "There is *dust* all over your dresser and wardrobe," I pointed around the room. "There is jewelry *missing* from the box," I noted. "Your hair is matted and unkempt, showing *neglect*. Your meal," I pointed out, noting the staleness of the bread and the sourness of the soup. "This is the same soup we had *last week*, and they have served this to you for *your breakfast*. I can assure you that they aren't eating this same soup themselves! Furthermore, you are wearing a gown with sweat stains, showing that it is *unwashed*. Your bed is unmade...and you have the ignorance to try to tell me that they have *taken care* of you? *Good* care, no less?"

"But I—"

"On top of all this, they have bullied and gossiped about you? Kathryn, *you* are the marchioness of this manner. You are the madam, and you now are carrying the heir of the Marquess in your belly. You *outrank* these simpletons. Must I really spell this out for you?"

She looked at me in horror as she actually looked around the room. "I...I am used to such things, marquess, I am not bothered."

"You should not be *used* to such treatment!" I shouted. "Whether it be here or at your former home, this is unacceptable for the wife of a marquess, or the daughter of another marquess. How is it that such behavior was excusable to you?" I glanced back at the butler. "See to it that they are sent to prison, after lashings."

The guards drug the maids away as they cried and begged for forgiveness, and I turned my attention back to Kathryn.

"*You are my wife*...and you are *carrying my child*. You are the daughter of a marquess. You are above such treatments. Do you understand?"

She gazed up at me with surprise, her eyes sparkling with awe as I had rose up to defend her.

I glanced to the butler again. "I expect to be the first informed if such behavior is shown to my marchioness again, or you will lose your head. Is that clear?"

"I extend my deepest apologies for not having been paying close enough attention to her care, my lord. I had entrusted her to the head maid, but I see now the error of that decision. I shall look after her care personally from now on, to forego any mistakes, marquess. I will no longer leave her care to the maids alone."

"I expect not." I turned to Kathryn. "I would like to...invite you to breakfast," I said, scratching the back of my head. "I will have the chef prepare a new plate for you."

She stared at me, still in awe, before she gave another curtsy. "I accept your invitation, my lord," she said, voice thick with emotion. "Please allow me to change."

I gave a nod, and I walked out, sending new maids to her room to care for her and bathe her and dress her, before I escorted her to the dining hall to eat with me.

Chapter 4

Kathryn Soren...

Blizzard's Reign, 1315 Imperial Lunar Year

Things had calmed a bit since the day that my pregnancy was discovered, and Kenneth had started to regularly eat meals with me and check in on my wellbeing through the butler.

He was much more attentive and interactive with me, much more so than I had ever anticipated that he would be.

He was kind, and though I had caused a lot of tension, he was patient with me and insisted that I be treated well and well looked after.

Butler Aaron saw to my care, as he had promised, and spent most of his time catering to me.

He was one of the more pleasant benefits of having come to this estate and becoming the wife of the marquess.

I was able to relax and eat what I wanted, and Kenneth spent most of his time on paperwork and running the estate so I only saw him for meals.

"May I ask a question, marchioness?" Butler Aaron asked me one morning over tea.

"Ask away," I smiled.

"May I ask why it is that you dislike the marquess?" He asked with hesitation. "I know it might not be my place, but he is trying very hard to earn your favor and to be good to you...yet you seem to struggle to open up to him."

"I...I don't particularly *dislike* him," I said. "But...when we went to his parents' estate, I hadn't anticipated that marriage would be the outcome. I wanted...I wanted to meet a man naturally, build a friendship and a relationship of closeness. I wanted an organic romance. I suppose I was bitter to be reminded of the fact that I was the daughter of a marquess, and thus, only eligible to be used for political gains. I had only just met Kenneth, and I wasn't prepared to enter into a lifelong commitment with someone I didn't know."

"I see."

"Not only that, but I had almost no warning of what would transpire. I've grown up in a society where a man even touching a woman is considered a disgrace on her value, and if he touches her without gloves on, her worth plummets. It is extremely discourteous, and yet, he was touching my bare body with his bare hands and...and..." I convulsed with disgust. "And it hurt..."

He looked away, a blush in place. "Yes, I can see how it must have looked from your perspective."

"I just...don't think that I can love someone in this situation. It seems unlikely to me. I don't hate him. I don't even dislike him that much. I'm just...bitter."

He smiled. "You never know, my lady. Things could develop between the two of you someday. After all, you two will live together for the rest of your lives. You will have children. You will be parents."

I considered that statement. "Perhaps. It would be good not to hate each other. I don't hate him," I said. "He might hate me—"

"You should try to give him a little credit, my lady. He has tried to give you as much space as you need, while taking care of your needs. And, you are expecting his heir to the Marquess title and fortune."

I gave a nod. I knew, already, that my child was the future of my husband's house. I knew that my child would be a high-born noble, just as me and my husband were.

It was a lot of responsibility for a fourteen-year-old girl to handle.

Rain's Fall, 1315 ILY

The marquess and I ate supper quietly, enjoying the outdoor garden as crickets chirped around us and flowers were in full bloom.

Maids stood at the side, along with butler Aaron, waiting on us to finish our meal.

Things had improved a lot over the months of our marriage, since the pregnancy was discovered.

We had both made a lot of effort to get along, and it no longer felt quite so forced.

I could honestly say that I didn't hate being here, anymore. It was still not as pleasant as I would have liked, and I wasn't in love with Kenneth, but...I could feel his efforts to treat me well, and take an active role in my pregnancy. He was very excited at the prospect of bringing a baby into the home, even though we were so young.

It just took a lot of pressure off of us to have children in the future, and meant that we could grow a more...organic connection later on, rather than force ourselves to be intimate without one.

I appreciated his consideration, and we threw ourselves into preparation and excitement for the arrival of our child.

I gasped, feeling my baby moving gently in my swelling belly. I was due to give birth in just over three months, and so the baby was a fairly good size and was quite active now.

"Madam?" I heard my husband ask, and I glanced at him as he watched me with concern. "Are you alright?"

He had started addressing me formally anytime we were around anyone else, because we'd had another incident with the maids not respecting me due to his lack of care in how he regarded me before.

Now, he addressed me formally and I finally had started to gain the respect of the maids of this estate because he, himself, showed me respect as his wife. It was still work in progress, but the new title was helping to remind them of their place.

No matter what they thought, I was the marchioness. I still had difficulties acting like one, but I was taking a lesson from my husband and the butler on keeping the maids in line.

"The baby is kicking," I smiled, and he looked at me in surprise.

"May...may I feel it?" He asked, surprising me.

"Of course, my lord. It is your child," I said, soft, and he came to kneel beside my seat as he lay his hand on my belly, feeling for the kick.

I gasped again as the baby kicked directly beneath where his hand rested, and his face lit up as he felt it.

"That is amazing!" He said, laughing. "That...that's my baby in there," he said, gentle. "I will be honest; I hadn't really felt that it was real until now. It really is real! It's really real!" He laughed.

"Yes," I smiled. "It is really real."

"I have to admit to you, that it hadn't seemed like it. It seemed far away, like a distant dream. But now, feeling it move inside of you, kicking and growing...it feels a lot more real to me, now." He smiled up at me. "Thank you, madam...thank you for this child." He took my hand, pressing a kiss to the back of my hand. "I may not ever be in love with you, but I promise to respect you and honor your position."

Tears welled up in my eyes, and I smiled. "Thank you...Kenneth."

Solaris's Gifts, 1315 SLY

"Hurrah!" The crowd of ladies cheered in the women's drawing room, giving me gifts, and congratulating me, baby shower in full swing.

The husbands of all of these ladies had gathered in the men's drawing room for drinks and cigars, celebrating in their own way, as tradition deemed for our society.

I took a deep breath, lifting myself out of my chair and making my way out to the terrace, taking in some much-needed fresh air.

I hadn't ever been one for crowds, and I wondered how that would affect my social debut when I turned sixteen.

When a woman made her social debut at sixteen and entered high society, she was expected to attend banquets, tea-parties, luncheons, and all sorts of fundraising events in order to gain a good reputation and bring up well-mannered, well-socialized children in order to gain a stronger foothold in the higher circles.

Being well-liked at these events could make all the difference between your child gaining a good marriage partner, or a partner who wouldn't benefit well at all.

Anything less than graceful eloquence was considered ill-bred and lowly, dissociable, ill-mannered, and to be shunned.

After all, social status was very important when arranging your connections to other high-status families.

I sighed, looking among the flowers of the garden, restless.

"Are you alright, miss—" I turned at the voice, and I saw my brother-in-law, Killian, standing there, bringing me a parasol. "Oh, madam," he smiled, giving a small bow at the waist. "I am sorry, I didn't recognize you from where I was standing."

I smiled, giving a curtsy. "It is quite alright, Lord Killian."

"Are you alright, though?" He asked. "It seems you are missing your party, and you don't look very well…"

"I had to get some fresh air," I said, stroking my belly and looking back out over the gardens. "I have to admit, I am not very good with crowds…all of this…" I sighed. "It…is a lot to take in." I gasped, suddenly realizing how unethical it was to complain to a lord in this manner. "Oh, please, do excuse me! I beg your pardon," I said, but he waved it off, an easygoing grin in place.

"Please, at ease, sister-in-law," he smiled. "I understand…you are so young; it must seem like a lot of responsibility to be thrown into all at once."

I gave a nod. "It does."

He held the parasol over me, being sure to keep me in the shade. "Be careful of being in this heat too much, madam. You could make yourself sick. I wouldn't wish for you to fall ill, sister-in-law."

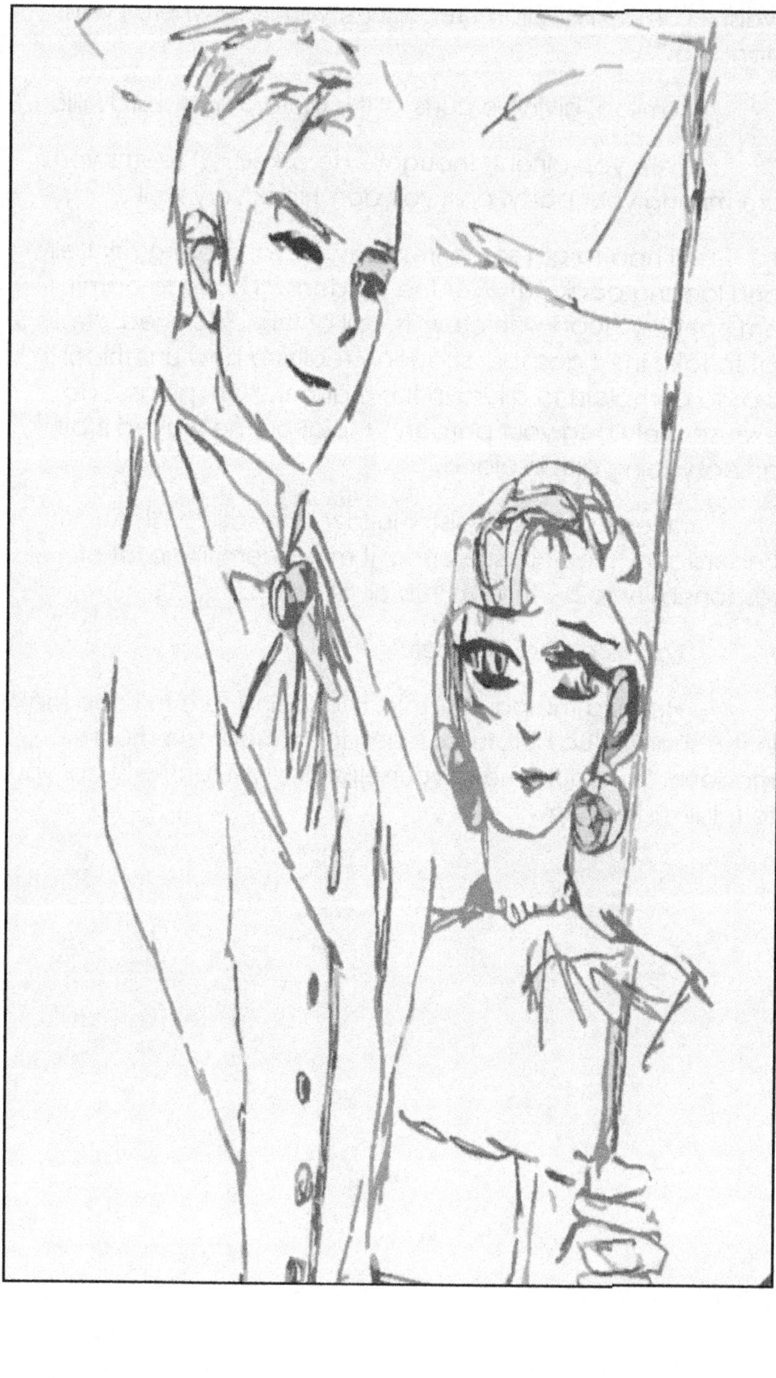

I smiled. "Thank you for your consideration, Lord Killian."

"Please, don't hesitate to reach out if you ever need anything. We are family, after all. And I cannot wait to meet my darling niece or nephew." He gave a bow, and handed me the parasol before he went back into the door that led to the men's drawing room nearby.

I smiled after him.

It wasn't so bad, being part of this family. I could count on them for my child.

Solaris's Reign, 1315 ILY

It was the tenth day of the month, when I suddenly felt strong contractions and my water broke.

Thankfully, Kenneth had employed a physician to stay in residence on the estate in case I went into labor, so the maids rushed and scurried to get me set up in a room and bring the doctor to me at once.

I cried out and sobbed as wave after wave of pain flooded over me, and after what felt like a very long time and a lot of strain with pushing...finally, I heard a cry.

I gasped, looking for the source, and I found a body being cleaned before it was swaddled, and the tiny, squirmy bundle was handed to me quickly but with care.

"Congratulations, marchioness," the doctor smiled. "You have a son."

The maids rushed to retrieve the marquess even as I held my son, stroking his tiny red cheeks and taking in his scent.

My son, the future of the Soren Marquess title, had light tufts of blonde hair on his head, his eyes scrunched closed as he belted out cries with his powerful lungs.

He was beautiful, and I felt my heart shift as I looked at him.

He had been *inside* of me, created from my own body and that of his father, cultivated in my belly for nine months before he made his appearance.

I didn't know what love was before he arrived, but now, I couldn't imagine anything sweeter.

Everything, in the end, had been worth it.

His father and I may not have had the greatest start. In fact, it had been a nightmare at first.

However, we had grown to become friends, and had gotten used to one another. We were closer, and now...

Now, we had a son.

The door swung open, and the marquess strode into the room, a grin lighting his face as he came to our sides.

"A son!" He smiled, leaning forward to press a kiss to my sweaty hair. "You, my madam, have given me a healthy, beautiful son. Thank you," he smiled, before he looked to the baby. "Carson," he smiled. "Carson James Soren."

"Carson," I breathed the name, gazing down at my son.

Chapter 5

Kathryn...

Veras's Height, 1316 Imperial Lunar Year

Preparations for my social debut were well underway in being prepared, despite being several months away.

Kenneth and I had gotten to a very good place, lately, and we were even very close friends, now. He was an active father, and helped me with the baby. He spent a lot of time with us.

We still weren't active romantically, but all good things to come to those who wait, I supposed.

I didn't mind waiting, anymore.

In fact, it seemed better this way. With our having a son already to inherit his title, the pressures of being romantically involved were off of the both of us, and we were both free to just be friends and enjoy one another's company. I much preferred it to be this way.

Before, I had been so apprehensive and unwilling, but when I saw my husband, holding our son and cooing at him and smiling...I felt butterflies in my tummy, and thought for a moment...even a moment, yes...

Perhaps, one day, I could be *in love* with him, if that was in the cards for us.

I loved seeing him with our son.

My son was growing quickly, already nine months old and teething as well as crawling.

He had gotten his father's hair, of course, but my violet eyes. He had a handsome face, a stunning boy to be sure. I was sure that one day, he would be a totally gorgeous man with many women after his courtship. He would be successful and handsome, to boot.

Things were going well, and my relationship with Kenneth was improving.

Everything seemed to be going well.

There had only been one thing out of the norm, and that was...*my parents.*

They had only visited once, in all of my time living here.

My father and brother had come to visit, a week after my son had been born, to see him. My father had been very blasé about the child, and had spent the rest of the time talking to my husband about financial things...

My brother, however, had been harshly scolded for trying to converse with me when father had caught him on his way back out of the mansion. He seemed particularly peeved about something.

My brother had shaken his head and shrugged, unable to identify why our father had acted so...strange.

I had received a letter from my mother, telling me that I needed to start coercing my husband to help them by paying back my dowry and the money that they had invested into the marriage. That the conditions for their help had been met, and that we had wed, I'd had a child, and we were off to a great start. We were making connections. We were doing well financially, so it was time to pay them back...as soon as possible.

I had brushed it off, feeling that it was an insane request, but Kenneth...he had gotten very upset. He had gotten almost...panicked.

Had there been more to the letter than what I had gathered?

Were they threatening him?

He had rushed off to his parents' estate afterward, desperate to consult his parents about the situation...while I had fumbled with our son, crying, and upset and being rushed into my arms and watching him as he left.

When he had returned...the car had been damaged with arrows, and one of the horses were injured. I had rushed out in a panic, but he had rushed me back into the mansion, insisting that things were fine, and he was alright. It was terrifying.

Three weeks has passed since that incident, but I would never forget the look on his face when he had come back into the mansion...

He had looked terrified.

He had gotten another letter several days ago, but had burned it right away, and retired for the evening.

This time, he had sent Aaron to send a letter to his parents on his behalf.

Nobody had openly attacked Aaron, but he had made it clear that there were signs of him being followed.

Kenneth and Aaron both, however, had insisted that I didn't need to worry. That Carson and I would be alright. That we were safe.

They *stressed*...that we would be safe.

The insistent reassurance actually only served to make me far more panicked.

Sometime later, Kenneth told me late one evening, that Carson and I would remain safe...always.

It had made chills run down my spine.

I tried to put it out of my mind, though. Surely, he was right. Who would be after me and the baby? How could we possibly be in any danger?

Though, his constant tense posture and watching over us like a hawk didn't put me at ease.

He seemed particularly defensive and watchful of us, and it put me on edge...despite how much I tried to make myself feel like we were safe.

Much to my horror, and much to my everlasting regret...my senses were correct the entire time, and I should have listened to them from the beginning.

Perhaps if I had talked to Kenneth about how I was feeling, or perhaps if I had made them tell me more about what was going on, I would have been able to do something.

It was late into the night, mid-Veras's Height, when I was awoken by the sounds of crying and shouting.

Shrieks outside of the door to my chambers.

I sat up, rubbing my eyes and glancing around, taking note of the sharp smell of smoke and the increasing heat.

I startled, waking up fully when I noticed that my son crying in his crib nearby, and I rushed to get him in my arms as I looked around, noticing the smoke rolling in underneath the door of my chambers.

Fire!

There was a fire!

This couldn't...this couldn't be a coincidence. It simply *couldn't* be!

There was something more to this going on, I just knew it...though, in my panic and frazzled mind, wrought with being thrown immediately into survival mode and adrenaline, I coughed, trying to open the window to my chambers but not knowing how to get it open...the maids always did that, after all.

I walked to the doors of my room, and reached out to touch the doorknob...only to cry out in pain as it seared the flesh of my hand, and Carson began to squall at my sudden outburst.

I glanced around, desperate and searching.

How could I get out if I couldn't open the door...?

"Help!" I cried, but my voice was cut off by my coughing.

I was breathing in far too much smoke.

I pressed Carson's face into my chest, trying to shield him the best that I knew how.

What...what was I supposed to do?

I didn't know what to do! Nobody had ever taught me how to survive fire! In fact, nobody had every really taught me anything useful at all, to be honest.

"Help!" I cried louder, standing, and stumbling to the windows, beating on one of the windows and crying out to the outside. Could anyone see me?

Would anyone care, even if they did?

I started to feel heavy, and I struggled to hold onto my consciousness.

I glanced down at my baby boy, who was already getting still and was quiet in my arms...too still and quiet.

Only then did I realize that he was unconscious.

"Carson?" I cried, nudging him...but he was unresponsive. Breathing shallowly, but unresponsive.

I had to do something! I had to do something, try harder...anything to at least save my baby. Even if I didn't survive this, my baby had to live, at least!

I beat on the windows, though it was pitifully weak. I tried once more, beating weakly again, sliding to the floor as I started losing my vision. I felt like I couldn't breathe.

My baby started to slide out of my arm, and I tried desperately to hold onto him.

My eyes burned, and nausea spun through me,

How was this fair...?

My poor baby. He didn't deserve this.

• • •

I barely heard the beating on my door, as it was kicked open and I saw a figure rushing into the room toward me.

...Who...?

"Hold on!" I heard the voice cry, but it sounded distant, far away...

So, so far away...

Finally, I let myself go, and I slipped into a darkness.

I cringed as I awoke, pain radiating my body, and I opened my eyes slowly.

"W...what...?" I croaked.

"Madam!" I heard, and I looked to see butler Aaron rush to my side, lifting a glass of water to my face and helping me take a small sip. "Easy, madam...yes, that's right." He sighed. "Thank heavens you are alright. I truly wasn't sure if you would wake up again, but I did my best to take care of you."

"C...Ca..." I tried, but he stopped me. He glanced behind me, smiling. "Don't worry, madam, I know what your main concern is. Young master Carson is alright. He has already awoken, but he is tired and resting for now. I am so thankful that I was able to reach you two in time."

"Wha...?"

"The mansion caught fire...sadly, the marquess' body has already been found. I am sad to say that...he didn't survive."

"...Wh...what...?" I asked, my heart dropping.

My best friend...dead...?

"The fire actually started in his chambers, but that is the extent of what we know. We do know that it was his body, as we found his ring on his body. He had been asleep, and slept through the blaze. I had thought it was hopeless, until we saw you at your windows, and I rushed into the mansion to retrieve you. Thankfully, your room isn't far from the entrance."

Sobs ripped their way through me, and my eyes overflowed with my tears.

My best friend, dead. My butler, my sweet butler Aaron, had rushed into a burning mansion to save me and my baby. I was beyond grateful, and so touched. My home, however...gone.

"What will...happen now...?" I croaked out, hoarse.

He shook his head. "You are in charge of this estate now, madam. It is up to you. Though, it will take quite some time to repair things, and most of the staff have left. There were multiple casualties, sadly, and the rest lost heart once the marquess' remains were discovered."

"I...see."

"For now, I have set up a place for you in the garage," he told me. "It is detached from the mansion, so it survived without any damage." He helped me stand from the makeshift bed he'd made out of blankets, and lifted me to lean against him even as a nearby maid lifted my son into her arms.

We watched as the blaze continued to demolish the mansion, and he led me the garage a small distance away.

That was how, in the blink of an eye, I became a widow.

It was a while later, when I awoke to voices and the smell of medication.

I glanced around, seeing my hand being wrapped in bandages after an ointment was applied to the burnt skin.

"Good morning, madam," butler Aaron smiled softly at me, noting that I had woken.

"Has my family...contacted me...?" I asked. He startled, eyes wide, and slowly, he shook his head. "I see," I said, taking in this news.

Since I had my baby's birth, I hadn't heard anything else out of my family beyond those letters to my husband.

Before that, I hadn't heard anything out of them since I had arrived to the Soren Marquess manor. My father and brother had come to see me a week after the baby was born, but nothing before or after that.

I knew that my father was secretly glad to have me out of the house. All daughters were good for, after all, were marrying into other, high-ranking households to forge alliances.

I hadn't ever been particularly welcomed in my father's household. My mother had always looked at me with disgust, and both of my parents had always tried to keep my brother from interacting with me too much. I didn't remember why, though.

In fact, I didn't have many memories of my early childhood...beyond being punished with lashes to my calves from the crop.

Becoming a wife was all that I had been raised to do, and now that I'd accomplished that task, I was no longer of use.

"Have they heard the news?" I asked. "Seeing that the mansion is demolished...I am unsure how to proceed. Am I supposed to rebuild and stay here? Or am I to move back home, to be sent to remarry? And what of my son? Is he still the heir for the Soren name?"

He chuckled. "Yes, madam, he will still inherit the title. However, he will not become the marquess in title until he comes to the age of ten, since his father passed away and he is an only child. You, as the marchioness, and I as your butler, will be running the estate's business until he is of age to take over with advisors. As to your other inquiry...you may return back to your former home, if you wish, until we can get the mansion reconstructed. I am not sure if the news has reached them, yet, but it is only a matter of time. You are also welcome to stay here, and I will do my utmost to protect you both and to keep you in comfort and safety until the new manor is constructed with the insurance money that you will receive from this incident."

I nodded. "Where is Carson?"

"Lydia took him out for some fresh air," he smiled, mentioning my maid. "She has been caring for him while you have been recovering."

I smiled. "Thank you, Aaron...thank all of you, for those who have stayed and who are helping us. I know that many of the servants who made it out left, but it means a lot to me for those who have stayed."

He kneeled before me, giving me a bow, before pressing a kiss to the back of my hand. "It is an honor, marchioness."

Suddenly, we heard a car approaching, and butler Aaron stepped outside of the garage, looking on with a hand on his sword and a cautionary look on his face.

"Who calls upon the Marchioness Soren?" He asked, voice firm.

"I bring young master Luther Abraham, heir to the Abraham marquess title," the driver said, and I gasped, stepping out and coming to the car on unsteady legs.

"My brother," I said.

He stepped down out of the car, pushing back his ashen brown hair out of his face, his face pale as he looked at the damage to the estate.

"So...it was true," he said, sad. "I am so sorry, sister," he said, coming to give me a hug. "Are you alright? Are you, the Marquess and Carson uninjured?"

I shook my head. "I inhaled a bit too much smoke, my throat is scratchy and sore from screaming and I burned my hand...but I made it out with my life, and I am thankful. Carson...is alive, and sustained some scratchy throat from the smoke, but is alright and will recover. Unfortunately...I am widowed," I said, saddened to relive that information now, in its entirety, as I informed someone else of it for the first time. I sighed. "Where are mother and father?"

He looked away; a bit ashamed. "Father and mother stayed behind at the estate. They sent me to check on you and the damages."

I nodded. "I...I see."

They didn't even...care enough to come to see me?

They didn't even love me enough to come check after my safety on their own, after I had almost died in a fire that had demolished my entire mansion...?

"They sent me on my own, saying that they were needing to know if you planned to return, because we will need to prepare the guest house for you if so—"

"*Guest house?*" I asked, surprised. "But...what about my room?"

He hesitated. "Your chambers have been turned into a guest room for my new bride, I am sorry to say."

I startled, freezing at the information.

"What...?" I asked. "Your...new bride?"

He looked just as shocked as I felt. "You didn't know? I was wondering why you hadn't come to the wedding, but—"

"Not just betrothed? You...married? You already got married?" I asked, hurt. "You mean, the wedding already took place? But...why wasn't I invited? Brother, I don't understand! You are the one ally that I had at home, but even now, you...my room went to your bride?" I sobbed.

Butler Aaron came and stood at my side, a sympathetic look on his face as he reached up to blot away my tears even as they began to drip from my eyes.

"I didn't know that you were uninformed...I was so hurt that you weren't there! I asked father and mother, but they said that you returned the invitation and that—"

"Luther, father, and mother haven't talked to me since the baby was born, other than to send threatening letters to my husband! I haven't heard a word from anyone beyond the birth of Carson. Before that, they hadn't contacted me once *since I moved here*. They haven't contacted me since, either."

He gaped at me, looking away and pacing for a moment before he turned to me, eyes full of sadness. "You got *my* letters, though, didn't you, sister?"

I startled. "*You* sent letters?" I glanced to Aaron, and he looked stunned, shaking his head.

"My lord, we never received any letters from you," Aaron informed, looking just as befuddled as we were.

He looked offended and confused. "But who would impede my contact with you?"

I shook my head, scoffing. "To me...it is obvious."

"But I watched the letters leave with the courier!" He said, insistent. "They had to be stopped after leaving the house!"

"I don't know, but perhaps our parents sent me letters too, and they just…didn't reach me?" I asked, hopeful.

He didn't look optimistic, and I knew, then, that they hadn't written to me.

He would have known if they had.

"I see," I said, and he looked sympathetic.

"But you say they sent threatening letters to Kenneth?"

I nodded. "They seemed threatening, and after the first, he was attacked on the road. After the second, Butler Aaron was followed on the road. And the last…" I gestured to our estate.

"You don't mean to insinuate—"

"I don't know," I said, trembling. "All I do know is that they have never loved me, brother. And I am tired of begging them to."

He glanced at the maid nearby, carrying my son around and showing him the flowers nearby.

"I am thankful, sister, to see you and my nephew safe," he said, pulling me into a hug. "I was so afraid when the news of the fire reached us. You should come back home, at least until the new manor is finished being constructed. The garage is no place for a marchioness.

I let my brother comfort me, and before he left, I seriously considered what would be the best choice to make.

Finally, I made the decision to go back home for now. My brother wasn't deluded to how our parents treated me, and now that I was a marchioness and I had a child, I would surely have more say so than I had before.

I would be safe…

Right…?

So, I gathered what little belongings I had, and my son and I loaded the car with my brother as we went back home.

CHAPTER 6

Killian Jayce...

Veras's Height, 1316 Imperial Lunar Year

The word reached us in the earliest hours of the morning; the Soren Marquessate had burned to the ground.

Among the losses were about a dozen servants, as well as my younger brother, Kenneth.

I cried, hugging my mother as she collapsed to the floor in a crumple, and my father clutched his chest and leaned against a pillar nearby, gasping as tears filled his eyes.

"What of my daughter-in-law?" Father asked the messenger. "What of my grandson?!"

"Marchioness Soren and young master Carson Soren made it out with their lives, but they are currently unconscious and being tended to by the remaining few members of staff."

"Few members?" I asked, surprised.

"Most of the remaining staff left when the news of the Marquess' death spread. There are only a few remaining servants."

Anger filled me. They left the estate simply because my brother was gone?

What about his wife and child?

Were they not good enough to serve?

She was the daughter of a fellow marquess, for heavens' sake! The boy was the future of the marquess of Soren's title.

What were these people thinking?

"Alert us when she awakes and is in a normal state of mind," I instructed. "We need to find out what her plans are from here, and we need to be sure to protect my nephew. Who knows how the blaze got started in the first place? For all that we know, this could be a murder case."

A few days passed, and we received word that my sister-in-law's brother came to her estate to retrieve her, bringing her back to her original family home...though, I was concerned to learn of this.

If I was being honest, Kenneth had made it rather clear to me that he didn't trust her family, and that she was overly wary around him even after they began to forge a friendship.

He once told me that she often flinched when he went to hug her or touch her.

If he moved too quickly.

If he moved at all...

Meanwhile, we were preparing a memorial service for my brother, but when his own wife didn't come to the service, my family reached out to confront her about it, offended.

We came to hear, shockingly, that my brother's butler had been turned away from the Marquess Abraham's estate, and he had returned to the still-intact garage at the Soren estate's land, at my sister's disposal anytime that she was ready.

He was loyal to the end.

We heard that the reason she didn't attend was because she was physically ill, but when I sent a letter to the Marquess estate, I never received a reply.

I knew that she and my brother...they weren't extremely close, and she may not have been grieving in quite the same way that our family was, but I hadn't anticipated for her to refuse to go to the ceremony or to refuse to write back to me...

The last I had heard from Kenneth, they were becoming friends and getting closer. Possibly well on their way to increasing their intimacy as a couple. He seemed...content. He seemed to have hope for it.

So...why wasn't she responding to us?

Something was amiss about this. There was definitely something going on.

Solaris's Reign, 1316 SLY

My nephew's birthday arrived, and while I had expected to receive an invitation to a birthday party—or a celebration of *any* kind, really—I learned that the marchioness didn't host a party for him...of any kind.

Nothing.

I was rather surprised and perplexed, because she had seemed quite attached to the boy.

Perhaps it was because it was his first birthday, and he wouldn't actually remember it?

Still, it was very unusual for nobles not to host a party for every birthday...it was very odd.

Something rather strange seemed at work, though, as neither I nor butler Aaron had heard any word from the marchioness since she had gone back to her home.

I was growing increasingly wary of Marquess and Marchioness Abraham. They had reported as having sent some questionable letters to my brother, and suddenly, the estate burns down and their son-in-law is dead, and their daughter is a widow?

There were also questionable circumstances about my brother's body at the autopsy, and then, their daughter had missed the funeral. Their daughter, whom they had practically sold to our family, and was now single and living with them yet again? She should have received the insurance payout and started reconstruction of the Soren estate by this time, shouldn't she?

Why was she living with the Marquess Abraham? Especially when Kenneth had been so concerned...

Were they treating her well? Was my nephew growing fast? Were they treating my nephew well?

I was growing rather concerned.

Moon's Dance, 1316 ILY

"It *is* rather strange, isn't it? The marchioness should have sent out invitations a month ago to her social debut, but I haven't heard a single word about it," father commented. "Kenneth had already gotten it set up and prepared, and all she had to do was send out the invitations."

I had recently been thinking the same thing.

We had known that my brother had been planning her debut—to the point that it was already being talked about when he had passed away. Plans would have already been finalized for the social debut, but there was no mention of it among the other nobles.

What was going on? Something...wasn't right.

"Before his death, Kenneth had already started preparations for her debut, since she is turning sixteen in a few days. Surely, her family would have carried out the plans, in respect for his work if nothing else. I would have assumed that they would want her to be debuted and back on the market. There is no word, though. No news, at all."

"That is a common theme, then," Duke Jameson said, nodding. "We had anticipated getting an invitation to that event as well, since we have a daughter around her age that is well-liked and well-known in high society and would make an excellent resource to know, but we haven't heard anything. I knew that the Marquess Soren estate had burned down, but when she went back home to her parents' estate, I had thought that things would go back to normal for her and she would, if nothing else, return to the marriage market...?"

I crossed my arms, looking out the window. "I wonder if she is alright. There wasn't a birthday party for Carson, there is no social debut for Kathryn...? All letters are being ignored...? Visitors, from how I hear it, are being turned away?" I took a deep puff off of my cigar. "Something strange seems at work, here."

My father nodded. "That boy is the next Marquess. He shouldn't be neglected this way. We need to get him back, at least, and ensure that the insurance for the estate goes to his trust fund."

I paused. "Did we receive the insurance payment?"

Our butler froze, gaping at my father. "I...no. The check never arrived, but we've been so swamped with other business that I hadn't even realized it. The check should have been made out to the marchioness and sent to her...I need to reach out to Aaron and see if they received it."

Folias's Blessing, 1316 ILY

"No, my lord, we never received the check. I had been under the impression that the bank must have sent the check to Lady Soren," he said.

"No letters have been going through, though," I told him. "All letters for the marchioness are being ignored and all visitors are turned away. We need to figure out what is happening and the state of things with the marchioness and the next heir."

"I agree," he said. "But how do we go about that, my lord?"

"Have you forgotten who I am, Aaron?" I asked. "I am the heir to the duke—even Marquess Abraham isn't as highly ranked as I am. Nobody of higher rank has approached them as of yet, so I think it is safe to assume that he would let me see her, if I insist."

He gave a nod. "I hope you are right, my lord."

The following day, I arrived with butler Aaron and two knights from my duchy to the estate of Marquess Abraham.

When we arrived to the gates, the guards were stunned to see us, before they quickly moved out of our way and allowed us through.

"What is the meaning of this—" Marquess Abraham stopped short when he saw me. "Oh! Oh, L-Lord Jayce, what a *surprise*! We-we weren't expecting you, and certainly not at this late hour," he said, checking his pocket-watch.

He had me there, in a way. Even I had to admit that it was rude of me, what I was doing.

It was a little after four o'clock in the evening, and on top of which, I had come without an invitation and without sending any notice, so I knew that it was highly improper of me to behave in this way. The proper time for guests, other than having an actual banquet or party, was in the morning, before lunch time, unless the person asked to schedule an afternoon visit.

I was being very rude by even showing up at this time, I knew, but without any notice or invitation?

I was practically spitting on them.

"I realize that the hour and manner in which I have come here are improper, but it simply could not wait. I have come to see my nephew," I told him. "It has been *six months* since the fire that destroyed my brother's estate, and we've heard nary a word about my brother's wife *or* my nephew, whom, need I remind you, is the heir to the Soren Marquessate. I would like to know the reasoning behind this absurdity."

The Marquess sputtered incoherently, before his wife approached quickly, trying to mend the atmosphere quickly with her charm.

"Please, Lord Jayce, allow us to have some tea put on for you and make you comfortable after your long journey here."

"I do not care to have tea, I care to have my inquiries answered," I said, irritated. "Bring forth my sister and nephew—or is that too difficult for you to grasp? Produce my family, at once. Do not give cause for me to repeat myself again," I said forcefully.

She gaped at me, shocked at my crass behavior. "Why, I *never*! How could we expect to allow such disrespectful—"

"*Mother*," I heard a firm voice, and I glanced up to see a young man who looked quite similar to my sister-in-law.

I knew him, of course. It had been quite a long time since I had seen him, but I recognized him as her older brother.

"Young Lord Abraham," I greeted, nodding in acknowledgment.

He glared at his parents. "Step aside, father and mother. He is of higher rank than us...it would be wise for us to heed his request. Please, come with me, Lord Jayce," he said, and he stepped back into the manor.

I brushed past the marquess and marchioness without another word, stepping inside briskly without a look back.

Something was absolutely, definitely not right here.

I caught up to the young heir quickly. "What on *earth* is going on here?"

"I am asking you, Lord Jayce, to *please* take my sister and leave this place at once! I beg of you. When the fire destroyed the marquessate and killed..." he drifted off, and I cringed. He cleared his throat, moving on. "Anyway, well, mother...mother insisted that my sister be made into a maid once she moved back here, and took all rights from her to receive or send mail, receive visitors, or even stay in her old chambers! Father wasn't too entirely cross at the suggestion, so he allowed it."

I gaped at him, horrified. "Where is Kathryn?" I asked.

"She is currently staying in the servant's quarters, and her son is staying in a separate guest room in the estate."

"I beg your pardon!?" I gaped at him, halting. "Hold on, hold on, *wait*. Are you...are you suggesting to me that my brother's wife, the *marchioness of Soren*, is now a servant? Simply because she is widowed?"

He looked ashamed. "If it weren't for all of the mail being scoured through and monitored, I would have asked for help by now."

"...What do you mean?"

He sighed. "Father threatened to disinherit me if I tried to contact anyone again, saying that she would be allowed to reach out for your family once her son came of age to ascend the marquess title. Father, unfortunately, has never allowed my sister to have any rights here."

"But *why*? She is the daughter of a the marquess, so I just don't understand why she is treated this—"

"She is an *illegitimate child*," he said, softly in a whisper to where I could hardly hear him.

I gaped at him. "What...?" I asked. "I beg your pardon?"

"...It was recently revealed to me by my parents, when I had attempted to defend her. It turns out that she is my father's illegitimate child."

That, right there, could have been information that kept my family from accepting a marriage with her in the first place!

Her family had pulled a fast one on us, not telling us about her lineage before.

It was highly improper to wed a high-born nobleman—an heir to a title and estate, at that—to an illegitimate child!

If my parents found out about this...they could easily declare the marriage void, take my nephew from his mother, and declare her a fraud, sending her off to a nunnery.

Or, if they chose to go a step further, they could be within their rights to disinherit my nephew altogether.

They could marry me off to a high-born lady, and simply use my second son to become the heir for the Soren estate.

The young marquess heir continued. "She is the daughter of my father and a maid—"

Oh, *heavens*. She wasn't even the daughter of her father and another noblewoman!

She was the child of a servant...!

"Thankfully, she took after father in looks, so we always passed her off as mother's child. Mother, in particular, has always abhorred her, and father feels that she is a shame to the family. The only reason, it turns out...that my father ever allowed her into our family...was to wed her off for profit."

"...But why didn't he just do that again?" I asked.

"He thought putting her back on the marriage market would bring too much attention to her, and that's also why we didn't give her a debut."

I realized it, then. "Then...if my brother *had* given her a debut before he had died, her relation to your family wouldn't have been a topic other than that she was a daughter of this family to begin with. But with the fact that she is *widowed* and the idea of putting her up for another marriage publicly, she would have her full background dug through. My family didn't push for information because we needed a noble lady to marry my brother, and we were desperate and short on time..."

"Yes," he said. "That's why, when your family reached out to us for help for your brother, we threw her into the marriage without considering any other options. But now that she is widowed..."

"I see," I said, brushing my hair out of my face. "How shameful, turning his daughter into a maid just because he thinks she is too much trouble to deal with. It isn't her fault."

"*I agree*...but father and mother don't." He sighed.

"And why is it that you agree with me?"

He looked appalled. "I love my sister, Lord Jayce. I want to see her get out of here, and live a happy, peaceful life. It breaks my heart to see her treated as a servant."

"Oh!" I said, suddenly remembering a huge piece of the puzzle I was trying to put together. "I also need to know if her insurance check arrived. We never received it, and the mansion has yet to be rebuilt..."

"The insurance check?" He asked, stunned.

I nodded. "Butler Aaron is, sadly, the only servant remaining, because he was the only one willing to stay without pay. By law, that money belongs to the marchioness and my nephew, so—"

He startled, looking surprised. "Oh, *no*...No, no, no, no, *no*!"

"What?"

He rushed me through the halls, and pointed out the back window to the back of the estate...where a new estate was being built.

"Father and mother...they started crowing and cheering one afternoon, and *construction* began right away. Father said that the new building would be the mansion that he and mother would retire into, while I would become the marquess and take over the original, *historical family home*. The building we are currently in."

I gaped, suddenly realizing...

"You...you mean to say..."

"I believe it to be so," he said. "I can't actually prove it, but I am almost positive."

His parents had spent my sister-in-law's fortune, in order to build themselves a new estate.

"Those greedy bastards!" I shouted, and he looked solemn.

"I had no idea that it was *Kathryn's* money...The thought never even crossed my mind! I've been such a fool!"

"This is quite a conundrum," I said. "If I sue them...you will be affected, and I don't actually want that."

I could see him working things around in his mind. "I will be turning twenty-one soon, and I will take over the title. When I become the Marquess, I will put back the money to replace what was taken from her," he promised, holding a fist over his heart. "I will even put that in writing, and we can have it notarized. This isn't something that *I* can overlook, either. She was legally due that money, via the death of her husband. That wasn't money that father and mother could take from her."

I nodded. "We will draw up a document stating that, then," I said. "I do not wish to sue the Abraham family and affect you as well, so if you are willing to do that, then let's draw up a contract."

He smiled. "Yes," he said. "I am more than happy to replace that. I will become the marquess when I turn twenty-one, which is only a few years away."

I nodded. "Until then...I will allow Kathryn and Carson to stay at my personal estate."

He nodded. "Please...get her out of here quickly. I fear father and mother may start a fit over it, but—"

"Let them try. I am the duke-to-be. Watch me. Now...lead on."

He led me once more through the halls of the estate, and finally, we reached the hall that the servants were housed in.

The servants there gaped at us, as we strode confidently through their area, until we stopped at a door at the very end.

Luther knocked, and after a moment, the door cracked open just slightly.

When I saw her, I struggled to keep my jaw from dropping.

She had lost a considerable amount of weight since I had seen her last.

It had been a while, but there was no way the change should have been this jarring...

Her cheeks sunk in a little, and she had bags under her eyes.

She had a bandage on her forehead that was tinged red from a fresh wound, and her hands were scratched up and full of blisters. Her uniform hung loosely on her, and it was dirty and ragged.

"*Kathryn?*" I asked, gaping.

She flinched hard, and slowly, shakily turned her head in my direction. "K...Killian?" She asked, sallow face horrified.

She rushed to shut the door, but I pushed on it, nudging her out of the way and looked around her quarters.

There was a simple, dingy mattress on the floor, and a bucket to relieve herself in. There was a small, torn sheet on the mattress that served as her bed, and one extra change of maid's clothing on the chair nearby.

"What...you aren't even allowed to use the toilet?" I asked, enraged.

She glanced away. "The other servants do not like having to share the bathroom with me. They poke fun at me; '*the girl who never should have been a lady is finally a servant.*'"

Rage boiled beneath my blood. "So, you just take that?" I asked, surprised. "You are the wife of a marquess! You are a *marchioness!* What is this madness?"

She looked away, twisting the bottom of her apron in her hands. "You mean I *was*, before he died...and even then...even then, I wasn't treated that way in my own home. Kenneth was the one who had to keep the staff in line, in order to get me any respect. Alone, I...I'm nothing." She sighed. "Why...why have you come here...?"

"Lord Killian is here to take you home with him," Luther said, and she gasped, eyes whirling to me.

"Wh...what?" She asked.

I nodded. "Yes, you and Carson will be coming home with me. You will no longer be treated this way—"

"But I—"

"Your origins be damned. It doesn't matter. You were legally wed and bedded by the Marquess of Soren, and gave birth to his heir. You are the Marchioness of Soren."

Tears welled in her eyes as soft, tired moans came out of her throat, and her hands came up to cover her face even as she sank to the floor.

"Do you have anything that you need to pack?" I asked, glancing around. "From the state of these quarters, I would think not."

She sniffled, and stood on shaky legs. "I don't have anything, but Carson may."

"I will go and prepare him," Luther said, and he pointed down the hall. "Meet me in the foyer, I won't be long."

I followed the hall back to where we had entered, Kathryn at my side.

True to his word, Luther returned within five minutes, a small bag of Carson's things in one hand, Carson in his other arm.

He came down the stairs, and gave the boy a hug before handing him off to his mother, who clutched him tightly.

"I know you haven't seen him in a few days," Luther said to her.

"*What?*" I gaped. "What do you mean?"

He hesitated. "Father and mother...have been having the nanny and tutors do his rearing. Kathryn hasn't been permitted to see him often."

"She is the *Marchioness Soren*," I said, firm. "She needs no permission to see her own son."

He nodded. "You are right...but they, unfortunately...do not agree. They refused to listen to reason, and confined me to my chambers for trying to bring him to her. I was at a loss for what to do. I cannot help if I'm trapped."

I nodded. "I understand. Thank you, at least, for trying." Then, I glanced to Kathryn. "Let us go, sister-in-law."

She gave a hug to her brother, and I shook his hand myself.

"You are welcome to come visit anytime...but your parents will need my direct permission to step foot on my estate."

He gave a nod. "I understand. Thank you, Lord Jayce."

We strode out of the mansion, and when Aaron saw us come into view, his jaw dropped and he kneeled as we approached, a sorrowful look on his face.

"Oh, my marchioness..." His shoulders trembled. "Oh, how sad the marquess would be to see you in such a state."

She didn't say anything, and only clutched Carson tighter to her.

Her parents stood nearby, and I glared over my shoulder at them.

"The Marchioness Soren and the young marquess heir will be coming to live with me. I insist that you have any of her mail forwarded to my personal estate...and if I hear that you have been taking any of her mail, there *will* be drastic repercussions."

The marquess gulped, and the marchioness looked away. Neither of them said goodbye or had a word to say otherwise, and I hadn't expected them to.

We went to my car, and I helped Kathryn up into the car.

It was a long, quiet ride home.

Chapter 7

Kathryn...

Folias's Blessing, 1316 Imperial Lunar Year

"You don't deserve the title of marchioness anyway!" My mother shouted, slapping me in the forehead with a crop. I cried, stumbling back, and dropping the teapot. "You clumsy fool!" She shrieked. "Clean this mess up! I expect there to be no stain on my rug, even if you have to scrub your fingers raw!"

She laughed as she stepped away, and I sighed, rushing to get a bucket and a hand-brush, as well as some soap, and I rushed back to the rug and began to scrub up my mess.

I gasped as I cut my finger on a shard, but I didn't make a peep as I did, indeed, scrub the rug until my hands were rubbed way, worn by the water and wood of the brush.

I blinked the blood away from my eye even as my wound bled, and I hurried to clean the bucket and dirty water, replacing them in the cleaning closet nearby, before I rushed through the halls and to my quarters.

I arrived, and managed to makeshift a bandage from old cloth.

I sighed, looking around my quarters. How long would I be here?

Would I suffer the rest of my life...?

I started to cry, before I startled awake, gasping in bed.

Bed...?

"Oh, madam," I heard a familiar voice, and I gasped, looking over to see butler Aaron.

"Aaron!"

He smiled, bowing. "Yes, madam. You fell asleep in the car on the way here, and so we brought you to the guest chambers so as not to disturb you."

I glanced around, realizing that it was night. "What time is it?"

"It is just after midnight, madam. You have been asleep for about four hours."

So, I had only dreamed about the previous day, just before my brother had arrived with my brother-in-law.

I looked at Aaron with teary eyes, and he patted me on the back gently.

"Hey, hey, it's alright, madam," he comforted. "It isn't your fault."

"I...I should never have gone back home!" I cried, and I clutched onto him. "They took Carson, and they told me I needed to limit my contact with him so he could grow properly. A filthy, illegitimate daughter-turned-widow couldn't raise a son properly..." Sobs blocked my throat, and I cried harder even as he tightened his hold on me, patting my back.

"I know, madam...I know. Lord Jayce told me. It must have been hard for you."

I nodded. "It...it really was!" I cried. "I wanted to write to you, but—"

"It is all in the past madam, you have nothing to apologize for. None of it was your fault."

"But...but I'm the one who chose to go back, I—"

He shushed me. "Madam, you couldn't have known. After all, all your life, you were still raised like a lady. You didn't know they would change so drastically when you returned. I feared the worst when they refused to let us visit you, and it seems that it wasn't good. They are the ones to blame. You have nothing to be sorry for."

I sniffled, and he handed me a handkerchief. "Thank you, Aaron."

He smiled. "Come, now, let's get you back to sleep. Is there anything I can get for you? A glass of water or warm milk? A sleeping aid? Something small to eat?"

I smiled. "I was thinking of getting up and getting some water and left-over bread, but—" I paused when he gaped at me. "Aaron?"

"Madam," he said, tearful. "Did you...have to sneak water and old crummy bread back at the Abraham estate?"

I glanced away, looking at my hands as I twiddled my thumbs together, giving a small nod. "I...I did."

He stood, a determined expression on his face. "I will get you some warm milk and some cookies madam, you need not get up to go retrieve such a thing. You are the marchioness Soren!" He smiled, pumping a fist, and resting a hand on his raised bicep in a pumped-up posture. "You can leave everything to me, madam, I will take good care of you." He turned after giving me a bow, and left the room.

I smiled, drying my tears.

Too long had it been since I had felt any love or affection.

My brother had tried to sneak me some portions of good meals back home, but he had gotten caught and severely scolded a few times.

Eventually, I had turned him away, asking him not to do so again. I didn't like seeing him get into trouble because of me.

He didn't owe me anything.

I was just the child of the woman who'd had an affair with his father beneath his mother's own nose. I didn't deserve his love.

Here, it was different...

Here, even if I hadn't been close with my husband, he had still been my husband. His parents had reached out and asked me to marry their son for the political and financial gain they would get. They needed me.

On top of all of that, I had quickly provided an heir to the title, a son.

There had been undeniable benefit for the family after their son married me.

I felt dramatically less uncomfortable around my husband's family than I did my own family.

This brother had no reason to hate me.

I didn't feel guilty receiving his kindness.

It would take some getting used to, of course, receiving kindness again in general, but I wasn't uncomfortable with it coming from my husband's brother or butler Aaron.

I was the marchioness Soren.

Aaron returned a few minutes later, a glass of warm milk and a plate of warm, steaming cookies in hand.

I smiled brightly, seeing my favorite cookies on the plate.

"Oh, Aaron," I smiled up at him as he handed me the plate and glass of milk. "You are too good to me."

He smiled, bowing. "Of course not, madam. After all you have been through, this is the least that I could do."

I held out a cookie for him. "Please, have some."

He grinned, taking one. "Thank you, madam."

We shared the cookies while I drank the milk, before my butler took the dishes away.

"Is there anything else you would like, before you get some sleep, madam?"

"Would you, possibly, mind tending to this wound?" I asked, pointing at my forehead. "I tried to tend to it as best I could, but it stings."

He set the dishes down before he lifted the bandage from my forehead, and he went to a cabinet nearby, grabbing out some alcohol and bandages as well as ointment.

He set to work cleaning it, before he put ointment and bandaged it back up. "It will likely leave a small scar, but it isn't anything too serious. What happened?"

I sighed. "Mother caught me with the crop."

He gaped. "The crop?"

I nodded. "She often used the crop to discipline me during my etiquette lessons as a child. She returned to using the crop to train me as a maid, and unfortunately, she didn't care where it hit me anymore. Before, she would only mark my rear or my legs, but once I had gone back home, the location didn't bother her."

He shook his head, giving me another small hug. "I am sorry, my lady."

I gave him a hug in return, before he held the blankets up and let me scoot beneath them, tucking me in efficiently.

"Carson is still sleeping, as well, so by the time you wake again, he should be waking up too."

I smiled. "Thank you, Aaron."

He bowed, before he stepped out with the dishes in hand, and I sighed, sinking further beneath my warm, fluffy duvet, and enjoying the poofy pillow beneath my head.

I hadn't even had a pillow back home, and had only been giving a light, torn blanket to sleep under that stunk of dogs.

I prayed for the first time since before the fire; I prayed that this kindness would last, and that I wouldn't be treated like that ever again.

Morning came, and when I woke up, I pulled the rope by the bed, before Aaron stepped into the room, a bright smile on his face.

"Good morning, marchioness!" He smiled. "Today is a beautiful day, and young master Carson has just awoken. The maid is dressing him and getting him prepared for breakfast. Would you like to take your breakfast in these chambers, or join the Lord Jayce in the dining room?"

I smiled. "I will go to the dining room."

He grinned, bowing. "Yes, madam. Let us get you dressed, then," he said, setting down a water basin. "Here is some fresh hot water to wash your face, and I will do your hair before I lay out an outfit for you. Do you need assistance dressing?"

I shook my head. "I will just wear simple clothing, Aaron. I have gotten used to dressing myself, so it would be awkward to have you or anyone else help me, now."

He smiled. "If that is your preference, madam," he acquiesced quickly.

He helped me wash my face, careful to mind my wound from the day before on my forehead, before he laid out a simple gown for me to wear.

"Go on behind the partition and change, I will wait for you."

I did so, and looked at myself in the mirror.

I had, indeed, gotten quite thin. My skin sagged a bit, and my body was no longer toned the way it had been.

My belly was loose and flabby, still stretched from giving birth to Carson, and I was much paler than I had once been. My hands were still worn raw from the day before, but the skin was starting to mend.

I looked pitiful.

I sighed woefully, before I pulled on the gown and tied it in the back.

When I stepped out, Aaron smiled at me and motioned for me to sit on the stool at the vanity, and he got to work brushing my hair gingerly.

"I know how to braid, do a pony-tail, or a bun, madam. The more elaborate styles are difficult for me, but I am proficient in those three…or, if you would rather it down, that is fine."

"A simply bun, please, Aaron. That is the least likely to get in the way, and Carson is probably still pulling hair," I said, not really sure if he was or not.

I hadn't gotten to spend much time with him.

"Of course, marchioness." He styled my hair quickly and efficiently, before he clapped his hands once. "Alright, all finished," he said, admiring is handiwork.

I looked, and it was neat and tidy with nary a hair out of place.

"You are quite skilled," I smiled as I commented. "Thank you."

"I will escort you to breakfast," he said, and he held out an arm for me.

I looped my arm through his, and he led me through the halls and to the dining room as I glanced around in awe.

The walls were covered in rich, expensive wall-paper and panels, with paintings hung here and there.

I cringed when every single passing maid and servant we saw gaped at me. Multiple of them started murmuring to each other and glaring at me. I even...

I even heard one ask another why on earth I was here, and what was Lord Killian thinking, bringing his widowed sister-in-law here?

Self-conscious and feeling suddenly guilty, I struggled hard to not let my head fall and my sadness consume me.

I stopped just outside of the dining room when I spotted a painting of Killian and Kenneth together, rifles in hand, posing in hunting uniforms.

I smiled. It was good to see Kenneth alive again, even if it were only in a portrait.

"I miss him," Aaron said, soft. "I knew Kenneth from childhood. I was training to be a butler the first time I met him."

I smiled at him. "Really?"

He nodded. "Oh, yes. Spunky young master, he was, carrying a wooden sword with him everywhere, swinging it wildly and proclaiming he would be the strongest knight in the land." He chuckled. "I was much younger back then, still a young teen. I had just left my first mistress, and had come to the Marquess Soren to get out of being that old woman's man-servant," he laughed. "It was quite different."

I smiled. "I see."

We went into the dining room, and Killian stood, giving me a bow at the waist even as I gave a curtsy.

"Good morning, sister," he smiled at me. "You look a little better, and refreshed from your rest. I hope that you slept well."

"I did, Lord Jayce, thank you very much for your kindness. Your hospitality is truly generous."

"Not at all," he smiled. "And please, call me 'Killian' or 'brother.' You need not be so formal with me."

"Thank you."

"I wasn't sure what you like, so I just asked the cooks to go all out for breakfast," he said, gesturing to the large-variety-spread of food on the table.

There were pancakes with syrup and butter squares, sausage, bacon, eggs, cakes and pastries, fruits, biscuits, grave, and even salads that looked like they were freshly picked from the gardens.

This meal looked heavenly.

I took the plate from my place, but when I went to grab my own food, they all sat there, staring at me with surprised expressions even as the servants whispered, confused, and somewhat entertained.

"Oh..." I murmured. "That...that's right..." I smiled, even as Aaron led me back to my seat, taking the plate with him to the middle.

"What would you like, madam?" He asked.

"Just one biscuit is fine," I smiled, but they both gaped at me, before Killian shook his head.

"No, ma'am," he said. "You will be eating proper meals from now on, sister; I know you have been drastically underfed while at the Abraham estate, but you will not be eating so little here. Just eat as much as you can, and we can bring you more later, once you are hungry again."

I glanced at him, before looking at Aaron, who gave me a big grin and a nod. I smiled softly.

"In that case...I would like a pancake, some sausage, and a couple of biscuits with gravy on a separate plate...and I would like some fruit," I smiled.

Aaron smiled as he diligently got to work piling my plate high with food, before he brought it and set it down before me.

I set to work eating it, enjoying the rich flavors over the blandness of the leftover maid's food that I had been eating.

"Your chambers should be ready by this evening, and we have another chamber being prepared for Carson directly across from your—"

"I'm getting my own chambers?" I asked, stunned. "I...I am fine, Sir Killian, in the guest chambers. I'm happy to take a place as a maid, even, if—"

He cut me off with a look. "That isn't necessary, sister. You will never be worked as a maid like that again. You are the daughter of the marquess Abraham, and the wife of Marquess Soren...whether you are widowed or not, notwithstanding. You will have your own chambers, because you are not a guest. You are now in residence here; at least until Carson becomes the marquess, and the Soren estate is rebuilt. So, just say thank you and accept it," he laughed.

I smiled. "Thank you, Sir Killian."

We finished our meal without much more to say, other than a little bit of chatter over Carson's schooling and activities, before we were excused and I found my way out to the gardens with Carson and Aaron in tow.

"What beautiful gardens," I smiled, taking a deep breath of the cool, fresh air.

"Kathryn!" I heard my name called, and I smiled, turning to see my brother entering the gardens.

"Luther, what are you doing here?" I smiled at him.

He gave me a hug. "I came to see how you were settling in. I am glad to see your color coming back to your skin, sister," he said, nodding approvingly.

"Yes, I just had a very full breakfast."

He smiled. "I travelled for a few hours so I am getting hungry myself, but I wanted to be sure that you were doing alright."

"Yes, I am quite well here, so far. My chambers are being prepared now, and should be finished by the evening, apparently."

"Ah, I thought he must have joined you out here," I heard Killian's voice, and I looked to see him stepping out, his own butler in tow. "I see you found her."

"Yes, do pardon me for having the maids direct me, but you did say that I could visit at any time," Luther reminded.

Killian laughed, a bright sound. "I did, I did. I won't deny your visits with Kathryn unless she were to ever ask me to do so, Lord Luther."

I glanced at Luther, before I stepped over to Aaron and Carson. "I think I will take Carson to play by the fountain," I smiled. "If anyone would care to join me."

The day continued on peacefully, with Luther leaving so that he could make supper on time back at our parents' estate.

After supper, when it was time for Carson to be laid down for his bedtime, Killian directed me to Carson's chambers and opened the door. I gasped, staring at the room in awe.

Shades of blue were all over the room, with a good-sized crib in the corner, and there was a king-sized, luxurious bed on the other side of the room. There were toys interspersed around the room, with lots of children's books and other such things around for Carson to play with.

"It is wonderful," I smiled, taking it in. "What a lovely room. Thank you, brother," I said, and he jumped a little at the title.

"It is nice to see you refer to me as such, rather than 'Lord Jayce,' 'Sir Killian' or 'brother-in-law,'" he laughed.

My face heated with a blush as I saw his handsome smile, his dashing face blazing into my memory, and I quickly looked away.

What was I thinking about my own brother!?

"Come, now, I will show you to your new chambers." He turned after I got Carson settled into bed, where he fell asleep right away after a very tiring afternoon of playing, before I followed Killian out of the room.

He led me just across the hall, diagonally, and opened the double doors before giving me a bow.

"Your chambers, my lady," he said, gesturing to them.

I stepped inside, and I gaped at the beautiful décor; from the lavender placed carefully throughout the room, to the glass vases and trays holding gems and jewelry, from the beautiful violet duvet to the stunning crystal chandelier.

All of it was stunning, and I stepped inside, going over to the wardrobe, and running a hand along the cedar wood, freshly finished with a beautiful, dark-rosy lacquer.

Nearby were a few sitting chairs upholstered with lavender and violet embroidered fabric with cedar wood as their build, and a cedar coffee table with several tea cups and a matching kettle sat.

A beautiful, cedar bookshelf was in the corner of the room, filled with pink and purple covered novels to read; romance, obviously, from the look of them.

The cedar of the bedframe and bedposts, and the beautiful, plum-colored sheer fabric that swept down to close around the bed to offer a bit of privacy…

It was so much to take in, and tears ran down my face.

"It is so beautiful," I gasped. "Twice the size of my room back home, and even bigger than my room at the marquess mansion…" I turned to Killian, rushing to embrace him, stunned and stiff but gradually chuckling and wrapping his arms around me in a friendly hug.

"I am glad you are pleased," he said. "And look, look," he said, excited. "Your chambers are already stocked with clothes and books, but of course you just need let me know if you need anything and I will get you whatever you need right away. This is just the basics, so please let me know your preferences."

I glanced inside of the wardrobe, taking note of the beautiful, elaborate clothes hung there.

"You...really thought of everything."

"I did try, though I feel like it needs your own personal touch. As I said, please let me know right away if you desire anything."

"Thank you..."

"This is known as the 'Cedar' chamber. I put Carson in the 'Oak' chamber, and I am further down the hall, at the end, in the 'Mahogany' chamber. If you need anything, please let me know."

As he turned to walk out, I lightly grabbed his jacket sleeve, and he paused, turning to look at me over his shoulder.

"I...appreciate this, so much, from the bottom of my heart."

He smiled at me, turning, and giving me a bow, placing a kiss to the back of my hand. "It isn't a problem. Goodnight, Marchioness."

"Goodnight, young duke," I said, giving a curtsy, before he turned and left the room, leaving me to myself.

I sighed, leaning back against the closed doors, gazing around the beautiful room that was now my own.

How things had changed in such a short time...

Only six months ago, I had lost my husband and everything we had in a fire that had consumed the entire mansion.

Then, I had gone to my parents, only to be made into a servant and treated worse than a dog.

Now, I was housed in one of the most beautiful rooms I had ever seen, in my brother-in-law's mansion, eating and drinking as much of whatever I wished, living life again.

It made the bad seem not so bad, if it was something I had to go through to get here.

Chapter 8

Kathryn...

Year's Fall, 1316 Imperial Lunar Year

"I believe that is it, madam Soren," my maid said, finishing up getting my gown tied in the back, taking a look at her handiwork. She smiled. "My, my, how lovely you look. I am sure the family will be thrilled. Now, if only we could do something about those bags beneath your eyes! But no amount of makeup can hide severe lack of sleep," she sighed, shaking her head with her hands on her hips.

It was true enough.

Most nights, I had extreme nightmares, and I spent most of my sleeping hours tossing, turning, and panicked.

My poor butler and maid were losing sleep, too, I reminded myself guiltily.

I was a bit nervous.

Today was the annual Nivis Solstice banquet, in celebration of the holiday, and we would be going about thirty minutes up the road to the duke's estate.

The young duke was housed in his own mansion just down the property from his parents, so it wasn't far away.

He would inherit the title and fortune soon enough, and would transfer over to the main estate while his parents would transfer to this estate.

This would be the first time that I had seen them since the incident.

Butler Aaron met me at my chamber door, and he gaped at me, a blush on his cheeks, before giving a bow. "Oh, madam, you look ravishing! You have gained enough weight to fill out that gown quite beautifully," he said, smiling. "Absolutely lovely."

I smiled, striding gracefully through the halls, arm in arm with Aaron, as he led me through the estate.

"Young master Carson is already dressed and out at the car, my lady," he said. "We were just waiting for you to be finished."

"Oh, I'm sorry," I said.

He waved it off. "Madam, it is natural for a woman to be late when enhancing her beauty. You are so beautiful that it would be hard pressed to be improved upon, anyhow!" He laughed.

We reached the front drive, where the car sat waiting, and as Aaron led me down the steps and Killian turned to take my hand to help me into the car, he froze.

Eyes wide and his face darkening a bit, tinging pink, I had to wonder if he was alright.

I had never seen such an expression on his face before, as we stood there in awkward silence for a moment, the air thick with some...strange feeling.

Aaron cleared his throat, before Killian cleared his own, shaking his head and giving me a bow, letting me use his hand to leverage myself as I stepped up into the car.

I saw Aaron whisper something into Killian's ear, but Killian blushed.

...*Blushed*...?

Then, Killian gave him a sharp look before he stepped up into the car, even as Aaron smiled with a mischievous grin.

What was that about...?

I hadn't ever seen the two of them interact that way.

It was a very quiet, somewhat awkward ride to the duke's estate, and the tension felt thick inside of the car. The air was thick with tension, but why?

Had I...done something wrong...?

Killian kept his gaze trained out of the window, looking at the passing scenery, and wouldn't look at me.

I had done something wrong. I must have.

My parents were right, I was just a worthless, lowly—

No. No, Killian was kind.

If I had done something wrong, he would have informed me. He had rescued me from my parents, hadn't he?

I trusted that he would be honest with me.

When we reached the estate, he rushed to jump out as soon as the car had come to a stop. He stepped on forward toward the manor, even as butler Aaron sighed, coming to my door, and holding his hand out for me.

I didn't question it, though.

Perhaps he wasn't feeling well?

I was feeling very nervous myself, knowing that this was the first time in almost a year that I had seen my parents-in-law. I hoped that they still...liked me.

When we arrived, the Duke and Duchess Jayce gasped, surprise on their faces when they saw me, and the duchess ran to hug me.

"Oh, dear," she smiled. "Welcome, welcome! I know it must feel strange...after all, the last you were here, we were gathered for Nivis Solstice all together...and before the tragedy. So much has happened since then..." She smiled at me. "How are you, dear?"

I pulled back, going into a curtsy. "I am well, mother-in-law. I hope you have fared well, also."

She looked fatigued, but her cheeks were rosy and I could see the rims of her eyes were a bit red. "Oh, just missing Kenneth," she said. "It isn't the same...without him here. I know the two of you weren't very involved, intimately, but he always told us that you two were growing closer as friends."

"We were. It...saddens me that we couldn't see where things would lead us, and that he is gone..."

She beamed at the side, and I glanced over to see where she was looking as she spoke. "But I see we have a new little one to watch over!" She grinned, seeing Aaron bring Carson forward. "Oh, what a handsome lad! He looks so much like his father, but with your stunning eyes."

"This is Carson," I smiled. "He will be two-years-old, soon enough."

"Killian, my boy!" I heard the duke say, going to clap a hand on is shoulder and bring him into a hug. "You didn't tell us that the marchioness would be riding with you!"

Killian cleared his throat, looking away awkwardly for a moment. "That's right, I haven't had time to tell the two of you about what's happened quite yet. Actually, about the Marchioness...The marchioness is currently residing at my residence," Killian said.

They gaped at him for a moment, before the duchess directed me into the dining room while the duke directed Killian to his office to...*talk*.

I suddenly reprimanded myself for ever having thought that this was alright. I scolded myself for ever thinking that things would get better, and that we had a bright future ahead.

I had already gotten my brother-in-law in trouble...

I knew what they would be discussing; how it wasn't "proper" for an unmarried, widowed woman to stay in the same mansion as a bachelor who wasn't even engaged, let alone married.

It was likely that his father was strongly advising him to send me away, to send me back to my parents or to the marquess estate.

The duchess cleared her throat, motioning for me to sit down. She assured me that they were just surprised, that whatever had brought me to Killian's mansion must be important.

We waited a few minutes, before the duke and Killian came back into the room, somber looks on their faces. The duke whispered something into the duchess' ear, and she gaped, her face paling a bit.

...How much had Killian told him?

Did he know I was a maid, now?

Did he know how my parents really saw me?

Shame filled my belly, but I strove my hardest not to get depressed. This was the family's annual Nivis solstice celebration, and they were already depressed with the absence of their son, Kenneth.

I didn't need to ruin it with my own feelings.

Once everyone was seated, we began eating supper after it was prayed over and blessed, and I smiled at my son as he happily munched away on his dinner.

I glanced at Killian just in passing, only to feel my heart race when I saw his eyes meet already resting on me.

He quickly looked away, looking to his plate, and taking a bite before sipping his wine.

I thought it odd, his behavior.

Did I look strange? Have food on my face?

Why was he being so weird?

I knew that Killian hadn't seen me so dressed up before. Even at my wedding to his brother, I had been dressed modestly and well-covered, hiding my body to keep my chastity.

Then, at the baby shower, I had been wearing a flowy, modest gown that was comfortable but still kept me covered.

Now, though, I currently wore a womanlier gown; a heart-shaped neckline with the shoulders falling beneath my shoulder, and a sheer, thin fabric covered my shoulders and collar as well as my arms.

The bodice was tight and form-fitting, and the bottom of the gown flowed out in a smooth A-line shape.

The gown itself was a beautiful plum color, with maroon colored embroidery and lace over the gown. The sheer fabric over my shoulders and arms was maroon, also.

My hair was swept up into a rich, beautifully braided bun, a fine ruby pendant that Kenneth had gifted me in my hair.

It had been found in the safe, saved from the fire...thankfully, so had his pocket-watch and a beautiful silver and sapphire necklace.

I wore light powder over my face, and my eyes were darkened with liner and an agent to thicken and plump my lashes. I wore a red rouge on my lips.

I looked like a woman, rather than the sixteen-year-old girl that I was, even despite the light purple circles beneath my tired, slightly-puffy eyes.

My maids had been proud of their work, after I had requested that they make me look like a powerful marchioness.

We ate our meal peacefully, enjoying the serene joy of my son as he giggled and poked at his pudding for dessert, before we all adjourned to the parlor for gifts and cocoa.

Most of the gifts were labeled for Carson, but there was a gift for me from the duke and duchess; a coral-colored shawl, with beautiful golden embroidery of leaves all over it.

I had gotten the duchess a beautifully knitted, violet-colored scarf, and the duke a new, wool-lined coat and a top-hat, as well as a nicely carved, sturdy cedar cane. Thankfully, Killian had rush-ordered the gifts on my behalf, and insisted on helping me cover the cost. He knew that I wanted a family, and his family was obviously the only family in which I could have the opportunity with.

He was so kind...

Killian came and brought me a gift, and I was surprised at the gesture.

He'd already gifted me more than enough, giving me a place to stay, as it were.

I opened the dress-box, and I gasped at the beautiful, lavender colored, floor-length sundress with beautiful, deep purple lace shaped into flowers was stitched onto the dress. It came with a sheer, fine, purple lace shawl and a white sunhat with lavender and purple flowers pinned onto it. a beautiful pair of deep purple flats accompanied it.

A beautiful, thoughtful gift for the upcoming Veras and Solaris.

"I thought, since you like the gardens so much, you would be wanting to spend your time outside more this coming Veras and Solaris season, so I got this for you ahead of time. Since your birthday doesn't come around again until the fall, it would be too late to gift it to you then."

"Thank you, brother," I smiled up at him. "What a thoughtful gift," I told him.

Then, I pulled out a small gift that I knew that he would love, handing him the small, satin pouch of blue coloring, and I watched him untie the string before he gasped, letting the gift slide out and into his palm.

"Is...is *this*—?"

I nodded. "It was Kenneth's pocket-watch, the one that was gifted to him at our wedding by your father. I...I felt that you should have it, and that it should stay in the family. I found it in a safe that had been undamaged by the fire, thankfully, and I thought it would make a good gift. Do you...like it?"

He stood there, staring blankly at the watch with wide, tear-filled eyes for a few moments, even as his parents did the same.

He finally turned his eyes to me.

"Thank you, Kathryn," he said, strained. "You...as his wife, you could have kept this, as a keepsake of him. But you..." He cleared his throat, and wiped his eyes before he continued. "My brother and I...we were very close, you know. He was my best friend...and we were all devastated when he passed away. To know that his memory can survive through Carson, and through this watch...I will treasure this forever. Thank you, marchioness, for giving it to me."

He kneeled, pulling me into a hug, even as my parents-in-law did the same.

It was a beautiful, meaningful Nivis Solstice.

When we were going to leave, Killian came to my side even as Aaron carried a sleeping Carson to the car, and he held his arm out for me.

I took it, looking up at him with a smile.

"Thank you, brother," I smiled, and his face turned a flushed-color as he looked out to the car, leading me out to it without saying anything else.

It was a quiet ride back to his estate, and as Aaron carried Carson to his chambers, Killian escorted me to my own.

When we reached my doors, he took my hand, pressing a kiss to the back of my hand.

"Your face has been very flushed since this morning, brother. Are you...alright?" I asked.

His face turned a darker shade of pink, and he let go of my hand.

"You just...look very lovely today, Kathryn." He smiled, turning, and striding down the hall to his own chambers even as I watched after him in astonishment.

He...was flushed because *I looked nice?*

I didn't understand.

It almost sounded as if...I scoffed, shaking my head at the thought before I could even think it, but somehow...

It was the only thing that made any sense.

It was almost as if...he was...*interested* in me.

I didn't have any experience. My marriage to my former husband had been an arranged marriage, and I'd never met any other men my age besides him and his brother and my brother, so...

Before I went to bed, I pulled one of the many romance novels out of the bookshelf and began to read, preparing a bookmark for my reading time.

Perhaps something in one of my novels could explain his flushed expressions...because I was simply too embarrassed to ask about it further, for some reason, and too inexperienced to know firsthand.

Did he...*like* me?

Surely, that couldn't *actually* be the case. We were in-laws! He was my deceased husband's brother. I was the wife of his recently deceased brother.

His sister-in-law!

Maybe he wasn't used to seeing me as a female? Was he just that unused to seeing me look nice? What had I done wrong?

I couldn't understand what was happening, and I couldn't figure out what it meant. I was too embarrassed to ask.

Nivis's End, 1317 ILY

"Do you even realize that you don't have to be here?!" My mother shrieked, slinging her tea cup at me. "You can't even make decent tea! You're good for nothing! If it weren't for you, I—" she cut herself off. "I don't know why you're even here. We could have raised the boy without you being here. Go back to your chambers."

I sniffled, rushing off to the tiny room I had been forced to stay in.

I collapsed on my mattress, wishing desperately to see my baby.

"Kathryn?" My brother knocked on the door, and I opened it. He quickly pushed a wrapped piece of salmon and a buttered roll at me, as well as a glass of milk. "Here," he told me, in a rush. "They weren't paying attention, and I had a few minutes open in the schedule, so I had time to bring you some food."

"...How is Carson...?" I asked, shoving a bite of fish in my mouth.

"He is doing well," he said. "Learning quickly. I am trying to make sure the tutors and nannies don't mention you...better they not say anything, than talk badly about you to him, I figured," he said.

I teared up. "Thank you, brother—"

"What are you doing here?!" I heard a voice shout, and I shut the door in his face and rushed to scarf down the food he had brought me as an argument ensued in the hallway outside the room.

I sobbed and flinched as I heard my brother get slapped, and escorted out of the hall by the knights of the mansion.

My door burst open, and I screeched out in pain as the crop began pelting me in the face and chest as my father swung it at me wildly, reprimanding me for turning my brother against them and making him disobey their orders.

I was informed that the act of giving me a little food got him punished with a week confined to his chambers, and his wife sent home to her parents for a week for a vacation, while I would be going the rest of that week without any food at all.

I lay there, bleeding and aching, throbbing…alone…with nothing but a thin sheet filled with holes…in the dark, dank-filled room.

I shot awake in bed, gasping for breath and clawing at the arms that held me.

"Kathryn," Aaron sobbed, holding me, and I felt my blood freeze when I saw the claw mark from my fingernails on his cheek. "Shh, it is alright. You're safe."

I began to cry, and he rocked me, soothing me.

Morning arrived, and I received a letter from my brother-in-law, inquiring after me after the maids had reported to him about the incident the night before.

A couple of months had passed without me seeing much out of Killian.

His twentieth birthday had just passed, and he had celebrated it quietly without much fuss.

In another year, he would inherit the duke's title.

Lately, I normally saw him busy pouring over paperwork and working in his office, up to his elbows in stacks of forms.

It was tax season, I had learned from Aaron, and to prepare him for running the duchy, he had been put in charge of managing the taxes and sending the papers to his father in a timely fashion to be analyzed before they were finalized this year.

That meant that he had much less time to deal with me, as a result.

As weather was starting to get nicer and get less frequent with the blizzards, I decided to go and ask him for something for the first time, as I was going stir-crazy sitting around the mansion without anything to do.

Aaron set up a meeting with Killian for me, on my behalf.

"You...wish to go on a trip to the ice-rink?" He asked, contemplating this. "Yes, I suppose that it would be good to get out of the estate and go skating, since it is open and the blizzard season is passing."

I beamed a bright smile at him, clasping my hands. "Really? Oh, that does sound wonderful!" I said.

"Though, I don't think that Carson is quite old enough for that."

"Oh...well, I can't disagree with that. What do you think of leaving Carson home with Aaron and the nanny, and we can go enjoy the crisp cool air ourselves for a little bit?"

His cheeks turned pink, but he kept an even expression and gave me a nod. "Alright, then. If that is alright with you, then we can go tomorrow morning, if you like. I could use a breather from all of this work, that is for sure."

I beamed another bright smile at him, thanking him and clapping my hands quickly before I turned, and I thought I heard him chuckle as I made my way brisky out of the room.

The following day arrived quickly, and I got dressed in a thick Nivis dress and coat with a scarf around my neck and a knitted hat on my head, pulling wool-lined boots onto my feet.

Aaron assured me that Carson would be fine with him and the nanny, and walked me out to the horse where my brother-in-law waited, dressed warmly.

I smiled as we walked up, and he gave me a bow.

"Good morning, my lady. Are you ready to go?"

I nodded. "Yes, I am. Are we...riding the same horse?" I asked.

He looked away and rubbed the back of his head, a sheepish expression on his face. "Buttercup is currently needing to get her shoes fixed and her leg is injured, so she isn't ready to ride yet. She should be ready once Veras arrives."

"Oh, I see."

"Is riding together...a problem?" He asked. "If it is—"

"Oh, no, that's not it. I just was surprised."

He smiled and gave a nod, before he easily mounted his horse, Reign; a beautiful black stallion, a large horse of power and beauty. He got into place, and held his hand out for me.

I took it, and he pulled me up into the saddle, sitting me in front of him.

He slowly reached ahead, grabbing the reins, and held on tight. He looked at me out of the corner of his eyes, smiling. "Hold on tight," he said, soft, before he pushed us forward.

I gasped, giggling as I leaned back against him, grabbing around his arms as he directed the horse to trot. I laughed as we picked up the pace, and he laughed with me when I cried out a laugh as we jumped over a fallen tree over the path.

"Are you alright?" He asked, laughing.

I nodded. Gripping his arms tighter around me, though, he leaned forward a bit.

"You can relax, I'll slow down," he said, soft beside my ear, and I felt hot all of a sudden.

Why did I feel so hot...?

Was this normal? It certainly felt more abnormal than normal, that was for sure.

He leaned back again, and I leaned back with him, leaning gently against his chest.

"This is nice," I smiled, and I looked over my shoulder at him. I was caught off guard by his flushed face, and I quickly looked back forward as I cleared my throat gently.

What was happening with us? Why were we so...awkward?

It seemed to be happening more and more, and I blushed more and more often when I thought of him...of his handsome, chiseled features. Of his bright eyes...His angular face...

Oh! Oh, oh no. Oh, no, no. No! This couldn't be right!

I was...I was *attracted* to him, I realized. That was why I felt so hot and fuzzy and warm with him, why I blushed more and more around him.

● ● ●

I was...*interested* in him, as a man...but that...

That wasn't right!

He was my dead husband's brother, that—

This was...

It was wrong...wasn't it...?

"There is the skating rink," he said, and I looked ahead to see fenced in lake ahead, frozen over solidly with ice, and he rode us over to the fence before he got off of the horse, helping me unmount the horse and pulling a couple pairs of skates out of the sack on the side of the horse.

He had me sit on a bench nearby, removing my boots and helping me slip on the skates and tie them in place before he put on his own skates.

I blushed at the act of him touching my legs and feet...putting my skates on for me. Tying them for me...

I could feel my heart thumping hard, my fingers trembling.

We walked out onto the ice, and he helped hold me steady as we began to skate.

Struggling to forget my feelings, I giggled and laughed, enjoying the skating, and he chuckled and flushed as he watched me.

When I met his eyes, he suddenly flushed, and I followed suit.

This...was this happening...?

What was this? What was happening with us...?

"You...flush a lot around me," I smiled, finally calling it to attention. This wasn't something that could go on being ignored. I fiddled with my hands, looking at my feet as we skated to the fence to take a break. "Am I...doing something wrong? Am I making you angry or uncomfortable?"

He startled, looking surprised. "Oh, *no*," he said, alarmed. "No, it isn't you! It isn't bad! Honest! I..." He sighed, looking away. "I...I think I just don't know how to act around you," he smiled.

I looked at him, taking in his bright, golden green eyes. "I...I don't understand."

He smiled warmly at me, and pressed a kiss to the back of my hand.

My heart thumped wildly like a horse stampeding in my chest, my stomach clenched, and I flushed hard as he looked up to meet my eyes.

"That's alright. I don't know if I quite understand it either," he chuckled, before he led me back off of the ice. "We've skated for a while, so and it is about time to eat something. How about we get back to the manor and we can get some warm soup and some cocoa?" He asked, and I smiled.

I tried to put this out of my mind, much more content to not think about it right now. I didn't want to think about this...

"Yes," I smiled, and he helped me change shoes again before we remounted the horse and began our journey back to the mansion.

This time...the ride was almost unbearable.

Chapter 9

Kathryn...

Seed's Sewn, 1317 Imperial Lunar Year

I shot awake in bed, and sighed, brushing my hair out of my face.

I had dreamt of the day that I had arrived to the Abraham Marquessate, and my son had been taken from me in the arms of a nanny as I was taken in the arms of a guard and dragged down the hall to where I would be staying from then on.

I had been locked in there for a week with no food, periodically beaten throughout each day to get me compliant, and told how worthless and unlovable I was.

I had been broken very quickly.

I didn't want to be broken again.

Though, somehow, I didn't think that I would be, staying with Killian. He made me feel...

He made me feel good things again, and he made me feel whole.

It was strange, really. I hadn't ever felt this way with Kenneth.

Even through the awkwardness, lately, I felt better now than I ever had.

Since the day that Killian and I had gone to the ice-rink, we had had a few awkward encounters, but I had been avoiding him, steering clear. My heard always rushed and pounded when I was around him, and rather than being upset, I was...

It was rather thrilling.

That made it all the more concerning.

Aaron asked me about why I was avoiding Killian, and I had told him about how I was feeling. He said that he understood, and assured Killian that I wasn't angry at him or upset, and that I was alright, because Killian had been asking after me, apparently.

Then, Aaron assured *me* that Killian would wait for me...whatever *that* meant.

Wait for what, exactly? It was all such a mess, and I couldn't understand what was happening. I was starting to wonder if maybe the servants who eyed me warily and whispered about how inappropriate my stay here was, weren't actually right, after all...?

I felt like I needed to leave.

I needed to get the insurance check and get to arranging for a new mansion to be built.

I asked Aaron to begin preparations for this.

Veras's Height, 1317 ILY

"Don't you think that something strange is going on?" I heard a maid whisper, irritated. "The air is thick and tense around the young master and the Marchioness. It feels highly improper!"

"I know what you mean. Have you seen the way that they eye one another? Why not just put a sign on your head, stating that you're after the brother of your dead husband?"

"She is disgusting," the other agreed. "To get romantically involved with your brother-in-law! Even if her marriage was arranged, it is still a dishonor to your husband's memory. She is so shameless!"

"Yes, she is. Who on earth pursues their brother-in-law?"

They giggled as they left, and I felt sick to my stomach.

Was I really that obvious in my feelings? It was true that I had feelings that I shouldn't harbor.

I had stopped trying to deny them, altogether, because I had finally understood what my feelings meant. I didn't intend to act on them, though.

I felt hot as I glanced up, without being noticeable, at the window of the room that I knew was Killian's office.

I knew, from recent behavior, that he often watched me out in the gardens with Carson and Aaron, and I blushed heavily as I began to realize that he was starting to watch me more often.

I came back to myself as I saw Carson playing in the fountain, laughing, and giggling.

I smiled at him, splashing him a little as he giggled, and he suddenly jumped up and slammed his body back down, splashing water all over my head and shoulders.

I cried out in joyous surprise, laughing and giggling at the coolness of the water drenching me even as Aaron rushed over to take him to get him dried off.

I glanced up at the window of Killian's office, only to notice that he was no longer standing there.

Rather, I noticed with a racing heart, he was coming out of the manor, towels in hand, as he came to help us get dry, grinning at us.

"Enjoying the fountain, are we?" He laughed.

I nodded. "Yes, he splashed a bit too much though," I laughed it off.

As I reached to take a towel from him and I grabbed it, I noticed his hand didn't pull back in…

Instead, his hand slowly, gently took a bundle of my hair, stroking it down to the ends…and he lifted it, smelling the scent before he pressed a kiss to it.

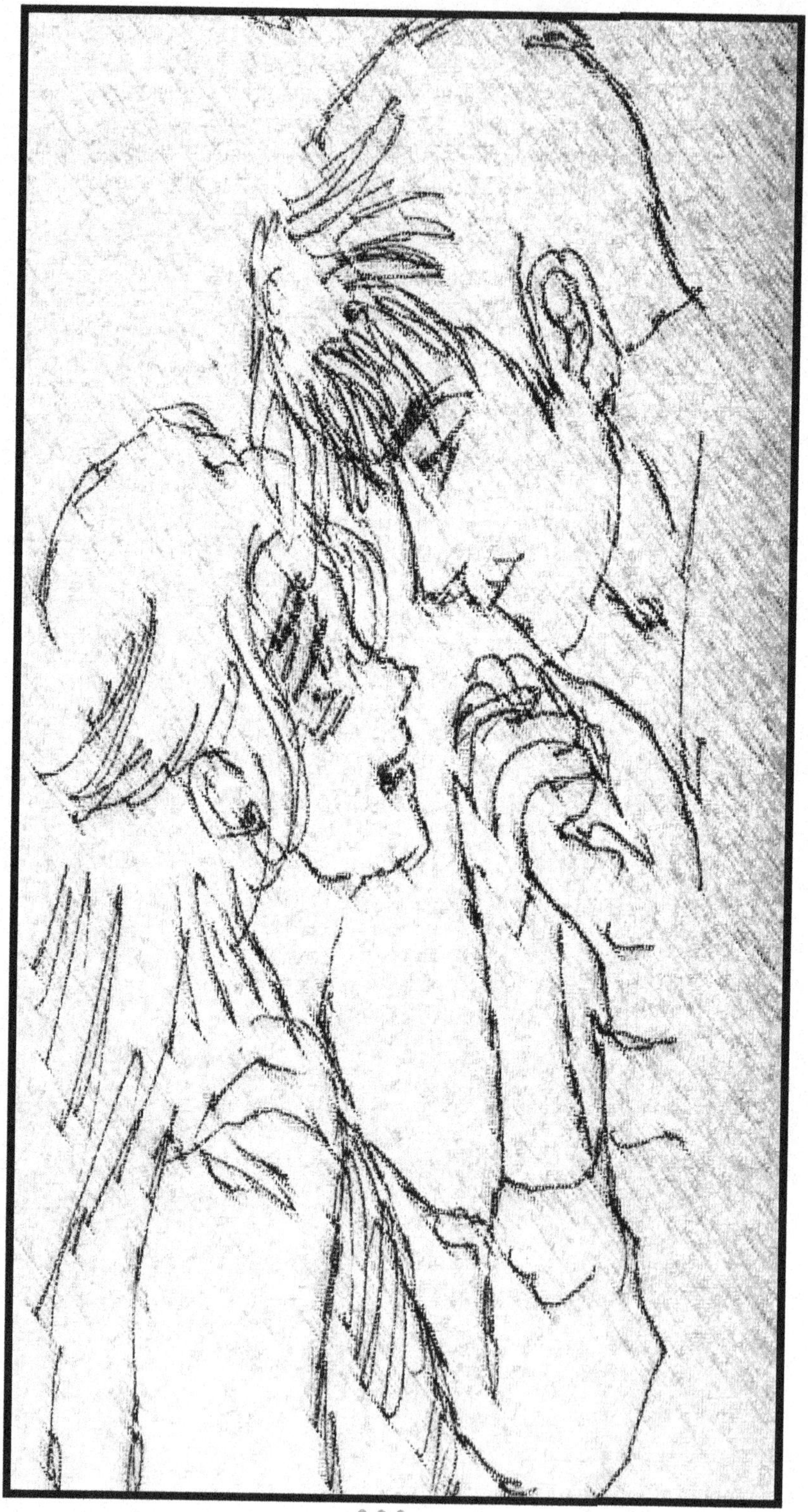

I blushed heavily even as his own cheeks flushed, and he looked up at me with shimmery, heated eyes.

I had still been leery and mindful of him since the ice-rink, but when he did see me, he had gotten rather bold with me, especially lately.

If it weren't for the reported trouble at the bank, and getting ahold of the tellers to figure out what the issues were, I would have already moved out.

It wasn't that Killian's advances were *unwelcomed*, or that I hated how he was acting...it was more so that I didn't understand what was going on between us, and it felt strange. I knew my feelings, and that they were justified, in a way, out of a sense of being beholden to him for helping me...but still...

He was my brother-in-law. It was wrong for us to become a couple.

My husband may have died, but it didn't change that his brother was my husband. It felt...wrong to feel the way that I was feeling.

Was it wrong, if I was widowed?

I wasn't even sure of the moral standpoints on this!

"Be careful to mind your condition, my lady. You wouldn't wish to catch a cold."

I smiled. "Thank you, brother," I said, fidgeting.

I had grown to feel...very *hot* around Killian.

Every time that I was around him, I felt myself feeling hot, nervous...even bothered sometimes, bothered by how uncomfortable I was.

I didn't want him to *not* like me.

I...I liked how I felt when he looked at me, especially that look in his eyes where his eyes looked like melting, golden green with his heat.

I felt...so adult, when he looked at me that way. I felt powerful, like I was taming a beast.

He made me feel like I was a true woman.

It didn't change my position, though...or our relationship.

I was so at odds on the inside!

He dropped the strands of hair, smiling at me before he turned, striding back into the manor.

"Killian..." I whispered into the empty space after him, thinking about his heated gaze again.

Chapter 10

Killian...

Year's Fall, 1316 Imperial Lunar Year

My heart pounded painfully fast in my chest when she came into view;

Kathryn...

She looked like a woman, rather than a teenage girl, and I was only a few years older than she...

She is a beautiful young lady, I tried to rationalize with myself. *Of course, it isn't wrong to admire her beauty from afar.*

As long as I don't act on it, it is fine. She is my sister! Perhaps only by law, but my sister all the same. I shouldn't...I should not be reacting to her this way. I just feel empathy for her, that's all.

That has to be it. I just feel sorry for her. We both lost my brother. We're both in mourning. It is my lack of experience with women that has me thinking this is anything more than a temporary infatuation.

I was quiet on the ride to my parents' estate, trying my best not to look at Kathryn.

I couldn't stop blushing.

When we had arrived and they had been stunned to see Kathryn, I had been called to father's office to explain the situation.

"What on earth is an unmarried young lady doing, staying at your estate? Family or not, Killian, that isn't appropriate!"

"Father," I said, sighing. "When I heard that she hadn't used the insurance pay-off to rebuild the Soren manor, I went to the Abraham estate to investigate the matter personally. They have been ignoring all of her mail and turning away visitors, but I brandished my authority to push my way through and visit her. I learned from Luther that the marquess and his wife took the insurance payment and have built themselves a second estate, while they took Carson from Kathryn to raise him separately as they forced her into servitude."

"...*What?*" He gaped, stunned.

I nodded. "Father, you don't understand. You saw how nice she looks, right? Did you know that only a month ago, she weighed twenty-four pounds less? That her face was sunken in and her belly swollen from eating mangy bread? She was being beaten and even arrived with a gash to the forehead!"

He stood there, staring at me. "But...why?"

I was about to take a gamble, here. He could get angry, and void the marriage altogether. He could disinherit my nephew.

Part of me knew that it was wrong to gamble with their fates this way, but I needed him to understand. He deserved the truth. We all did.

"Luther...he told me the truth...the real truth, about her lineage." I sighed. "She is the child of the marquess and a *maid*...from after he was already married to the marchioness."

"An *illegitimate child?*" My father gasped, appalled. "And they passed her off for a true high-born lady! The nerve!"

"But remember, father, we were the ones who reached out to *their* family, first. She just happened to be of the right age, of a good family, and we didn't know. We were desperate in our situation, and they took advantage of it. They probably never intended to marry her off, but when we came to them for her, they just saw it as the best option. A benefit for themselves. Then, once she became a widow, they knew that putting her back on the market would raise questions about her background, her lineage, and genes, and so on."

My father shook his head, slumping into his desk chair. "What a tiresome situation," he said. He glanced up at me. "How long are you intending to let her stay with you? You know that you cannot expect any respectable ladies to wish to accept your hand in marriage when you are hosting a young widow on your estate, even if it *is* a relative. You two aren't related by blood, after all. I hope you aren't entertaining any particularly...romantic ideas towards her?"

"It isn't like that, father," I told him.

He gave a nod. "Good. Then, I assume her parents have given up rights to her?" He asked, and I nodded. "And what about the insurance payment? Are you going to bring up a lawyer?"

I shook my head. "If we were to sue them, it would draw out a long time in court, they could possibly bribe the bank to take their side since they are so wealthy, and honestly...Luther was kind to her to the end and was against how they treated her, even landing himself into trouble to try to help her. I don't want to drag the family name and reputation through the mud and ruin his future. He and I drew up a contract that states that as soon as he inherits the title of marquess, he will reimburse the insurance payment directly to Kathryn and she can do whatever she wishes with it."

He nodded. "I see. Good on him, then. Was that notarized?"

I nodded. "Yes, father. I made sure everything went as it needed to, properly."

"There is still the issue of Kathryn, however. As her new guardian, it will fall to you to give her a social debut...since Kenneth died before he was able to do so, and her parents refused to host one for her."

"What...? Me?"

"She is your ward, as of right now. That is what we have told the press, to give a valid excuse as to why she is living with you. And it checks out, doesn't it?" He asked with a shrug. "She hasn't had her social debut and isn't legally an adult, so it is up to you to be her guardian and look out for her interests. That means that you will put her back on the marriage market, you will interview suitor candidates—"

I held up my hands. "Now, hold on, I don't think that—"

"Why not?" He asked before I could finish. "You took her in. You obviously felt ready to take her on as a responsibility. It is up to you to look after her and Carson."

I glanced away, a blush on my cheeks, and he froze, gaping at me.

"No, no, no," he said. "Get that blush off of your face! You said you didn't see her that way!" He scolded. "You are her brother by law. It is highly irresponsible of you to have taken her in, in the first place, but to look at her as a woman? You must be out of your mind. Stop it, right now."

I sighed. "...Yes, father..."

We turned, and he led me back through the manor to eat.

Once the meal was finished, we opened gifts, and then, Kathryn absolutely astonished me by gifting me my deceased brother's pocket-watch.

She was beautiful, young, vibrant, and thoughtful...so, so thoughtful...and not mine.

She belonged to a dead man.

My dead brother.

155

It was increasingly hard *not* to see her as more than a sister, no matter how much I told myself in my head that I could only see her as such.

I wondered, idly, if Kenneth had gotten to see this out of her.

What had their relationship been like behind closed doors?

He had been telling me in his letters that they were growing to be friends, but were they *really close*? He had seemed to have increasing hope for their intimate relationship as a couple, from how he had spoken...

The more primal side of me, the side that wished to become her *lover*...that side of me wondered just how far they had gone, how often they had been together...how many times had she made love to my brother, exactly?

How many times had he touched her? How many times had he been inside of her?

The picture of my brother's cock inside of her turned my stomach and made my heart sink.

I shook the thoughts from my mind, even as I pressed a kiss to the back of her hand outside of her chambers to bid her goodnight, wishing that it wasn't "*goodnight*" ...

The blush that stung my cheeks was real.

My growing feelings were real.

How long could I last without her, having to live with her in this mansion each day?

I couldn't bring myself to make her leave, but I needed to avoid her, because my heart was too prone to get attached to her...

Nixie's End, 1317 ILY

As we skated on the ice of the lake, I noticed how utterly free she looked; the wind caught in her hair, threatening to blow off her knitted hat, her scarf whipping about in the wind, her laughs tinkling with an echo in the crisp morning air...

She looked like some delicate fairy, and I was her keeper.

It had been going on a year since the fire that had taken her husband, and I wondered in my mind if she missed him.

Did she grieve for him? Was she in pain?

Or had they even been that close?

I couldn't bring myself to ask her, because I knew she would wonder why I wished to know...and I didn't want to tell her. Would she think that I was sick for lusting after her?

I had been going out of my way to push through an absurdly large amount of paperwork recently, as to avoid her, but when I caught glimpses of her around the manor, my heart skipped a beat and I felt warm.

Was this love?

Butler Aaron came to my office one afternoon, glancing at me as I gazed at Kathryn out in the gardens.

He chuckled.

"My, young master, I would peg you as *smitten*," he laughed.

I blushed, gasping, and turning away quickly to hide my face, and he gasped, gaping at me.

"Wait...*are you?*" He asked, surprised. "I had expected you to quickly deny it, as you usually would, but you..."

I glanced at him. "Well, I...she's a beautiful young lady, and she's thoughtful and kind, and very gracious...and modest...and quick witted and sweet..."

He looked on in shock. "*You are,*" he said. "You're positively, inescapably *smitten* with the marchioness! But..."

I shook my head. "I can't be. I know."

He went to respond, but I stormed out of the room before I could hear his response. I went to fetch my own butler, to bring me more paperwork to fill out and get completed.

Anything to pass the time away so that I didn't have to watch her...

Veras's Height, 1317 ILY

I was watching her again, as I often found myself doing, as she was out taking a stroll out with her maid and son, pointing out the blooming flowers to him. It was still a little chilly that day, so she wore a warmer dress and a shawl.

"Why can't you?" Butler Aaron asked, soft.

He glanced at the invitations on my desk that I had prepared to send out for Kathryn's debut.

I knew, that once the invitations were sent...it would be too late.

She would have a long line of suitors, probably, as her connections to her father and brother, to my brother and to me would boost her status and make her much more desirable among the lords of the nation.

A debut was akin to putting a woman out on the marriage market, if she was unmarried. Though it was less common to see a debut for a widow, it did occasionally take place when a woman was ready to go back on the market—especially if she was still young.

I didn't have to worry too much about her background being revealed. If I put her on the marriage market, as Luther and Aaron had pointed out to me, the Marquess would never disgrace himself and his house by admitting what she was.

In fact, I was positive that instead, they would do all they could to destroy the evidence behind her true status: an illegitimate child.

"You will have to be more specific," I said, even though I really knew what he meant.

"Master Killian, please...don't shut your feelings away like this. I know that you feel for her."

I sighed. "I can't—"

"*Why can't you?*" He asked again, firmer and louder. "Why can you not love her that way? Because of your brother?"

I gaped at him. "Aaron—"

"I know I am stepping over the boundary here, but Lord Killian, they only had *their first night* and she didn't even see him for the entire next month afterward. It wasn't until she was found to be pregnant—"

"Wait, wait...you mean...they weren't...they weren't close? At all? Even after they started to become friends?"

He sighed, looking away. "No. After their first night, they both agreed to never be intimate again unless they were truly in love, and that...never happened. When they found out she was pregnant, they knew that she wouldn't need to have any more children for a long time, even if it had been a girl, so..." he shrugged. "It isn't as if you're trying to pursue the love of his life. He cared for her...but he wasn't in love with her."

My guilt lessened drastically, my relief soaring through me.

"Oh, thank goodness," I said, taking a deep breath and steadying myself on the desk. "I...I was worried that I would be pushing my feelings on her in her grief, but if they weren't close, then...then that means that she isn't in mourning."

He smiled. "Kenneth...he wouldn't have been upset, I don't think. He cared about her, but he wasn't in love with her. He told me so, several times. They were just starting to be friends."

"Thank you, for telling me," I told him. "The truth is, I had been wondering for quite some time, but I didn't...think it appropriate to ask her."

He smiled at me. "Lord Killian...she stares at you quite often, too, you know."

"What?" I asked, baffled.

He chuckled. "I think you may be surprised, if you decided to pursue her."

Does she really? I wondered.

I glanced at him. "But...she is still legally my sister by law."

He shrugged. "There have been far worse matches in the history of the royals, my lord."

He had a point.

We, as a society, were just getting out of a period of nieces wedding uncles and aunts wedding nephews, or siblings marrying siblings, cousins marrying cousins...

We weren't actually blood-related, so why should it matter?

"But...how do I go about pursuing her? And what about my parents? Father has already expressed his view upon me taking her as a lover...he was against it, vehemently."

He glanced away. "I can't say much on that aspect of things, my lord. But no matter what you choose, I do have one favor of you, if I may?"

"...And what is that?"

"Just be gentle with her, my lord. Start becoming an integrated part of her life, joining her routine. Lord Kenneth...he couldn't bring himself to do so. After the initial bedding, he had left her alone, completely isolated on the other side of the mansion without him. She didn't even leave her chambers for over a month. But you...you have the chance to become a part of her routine. *You* have the chance to become something to her that he never could."

I took in that information, realizing that she and my brother truly hadn't been a couple at all beyond their first night.

I no longer felt guilty for my feelings...and I no longer felt a reason to hold myself back.

"Alright," I said, making my choice. "I'm doing this."

Chapter 11

Killian...

    A couple of weeks passed, and I saw her outside...she wore a sundress her brother had sent her for Nivis Solstice, so I wasn't offended that I hadn't seen her wear mine, yet.

    She was outside, splashing in the fountain with my nephew, and I realized that this was a perfect opportunity to insert myself briefly into their space.

    I wanted to integrate myself, slowly, because I had noticed that when I got too close, too sporadically...it had scared her off, and quickly.

    She had started seeking after her insurance payment to build the new Soren marquessate estate, even...though, I explained to Aaron very quickly what was happening with that, and he agreed to keep it withheld from the marchioness for the time being...just until we figured out what we were going to do about it.

    I grabbed a couple of towels, and just as I was reaching the doors to the garden, I saw him jump up and land with a splash onto his knees, laughing and giggling as he soaked his mother in cold water.

    She squealed out a high-pitched laugh, shivering a bit from the sudden cold, and I approached her with the towels.

"Enjoying the fountain, are we?" I laughed.

She nodded. "Yes, he splashed a bit too much though," she laughed it off.

As she reached to take a towel from me and she grabbed it, she noticed my hand didn't pull back in...

Instead, my hand slowly, gently took a bundle of her hair, stroking it down to the ends...and I lifted it, smelling the scent before I pressed a kiss to it.

I just couldn't seem to help myself.

Her chosen shampoos and body oils that she wore were heavenly, and she smelled divine.

I was a man, starved by her, *for her*...

She blushed heavily even as my own cheeks flushed, and I looked up at her beautiful, sparking violet eyes.

"Be careful to mind your condition, my lady. You wouldn't wish to catch a cold."

She blushed and smiled. "Thank you, brother," she said, fidgeting. I could tell that she was nervous, but her eyes continued to dart up at me and her cheeks turned bright pink.

I realized it, in that moment, that Aaron had been right in his assessment. She may not have even realized it herself, yet, but she definitely liked me, too.

I chuckled under my breath as I turned and returned to the mansion, quickly and decisively choosing a course of action.

It would just take a bit of time.

Veras's End, 1317 ILY

It had now, officially, been over a year since my brother had passed away, and we stood at the site of the fire, alone.

Aaron stood on the edge of the property, looking on from a distance, lost in his own ruminations of memory from that night.

I hadn't been on the scene, but I could see the event unfolding in their faces as their eyes moved about the scenery, widening and wincing, trembling...

They were still in pain from this fire.

Carson had been left at the estate, in the care of his nannies, and Kathryn stared on with a somber face.

"To think that I spent less than a year here, but *this*...this is where I conceived and birthed my son. My husband...my husband, my friend, he...*died here*..." She trembled. "*I almost died here.*"

I remembered the story from Aaron.

He had barely noticed her in the window, and had rushed back inside to retrieve her and my nephew when he and the other remaining servants had almost lost all hope of them surviving.

They'd had bad coughs for weeks from the smoke inhalation, and the doctor had said that they were alive only by a miracle, as that much smoke inhalation would usually be fatal.

Their lives would be shortened by it, certainly. Their lungs were damaged, of course.

The damage to their lungs would last a lifetime.

The damage done to her psyche would last an eternity...for she still had nightmares.

Carson, though he was a small baby at the time of the fire, still showed great caution around flames, even now.

They were forever changed because of the incident.

I still wanted to figure out how it had started. It wasn't a natural event; I was sure of that. Especially after the threatening letters my brother had received from Marquess Abraham...

I suspected foul play, honestly.

I saw tears fill her eyes, even as she clenched her dress in her fists, and I stepped over to her, wrapping an arm around her shoulders.

"He would be proud of you. You have stood strong for Carson, and he would be happy that the two of you made it out safely."

She glanced up at me from under wet eyelashes. "You think so?"

I couldn't tell you what possessed me, but I couldn't stop myself.

I leaned forward, pressing a gentle kiss to her forehead, and she froze, eyes wide and cheeks flushing a deep, dark pink.

"*I do,*" I told her, and she blushed even deeper.

"Brother..."

I leaned forward, my arm sliding from around her shoulders to grip at her head, pulling her into my other arm as I wrapped my other arm around her, letting my hand rest on her forearm.

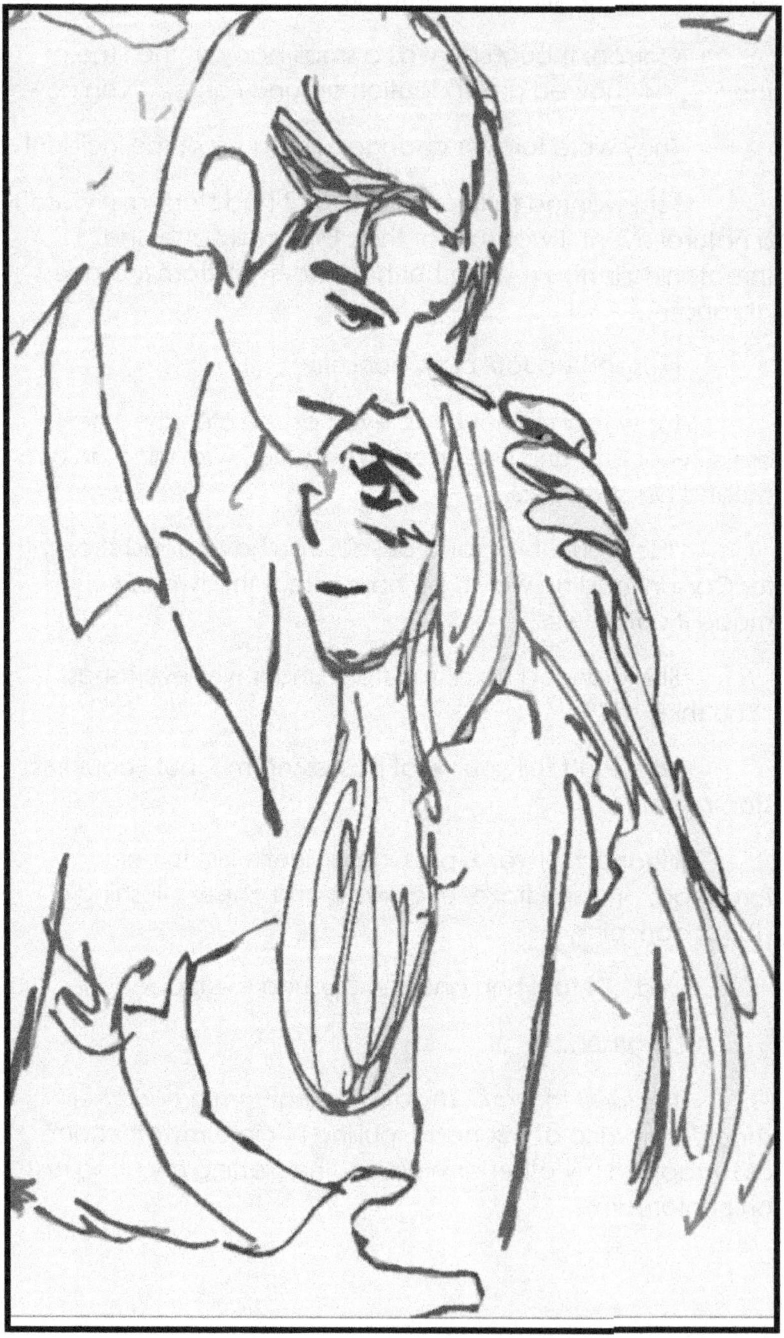

I heard her swallow thickly in her throat, and I could hear her heart thumping wildly.

I leaned down, resting my lips beside of her ear.

"How long will you insist on calling me by that name?" I asked her, pressing a little nip beneath her ear, and she jumped, gasping at me.

"I...I..."

"Yes?"

"I-I don't...I don't understand," she said, even as she stayed flushed.

"...Do you really not?" I asked after a moment.

She shook her head rapidly. "We...we can't do this, we—"

"Why not?" I asked.

"You...I am your *sister*!!" She said, alarmed. "You are my brother—"

"*Am I?*" I asked.

"Huh?"

"Am I your brother?"

"What...I don't—"

"I am asking if you truly only see me in that way? Have I been imagining your gaze upon me lately, then? Imagining your blushes when *I* look upon *you*?"

She gaped at me, trying to turn in my arms, but I held her firm. "I...we...but I...I'm a widow, your *brother's* widow, and it hasn't even been that long since he died—"

I paused. "Have we not waited long enough, then?" I asked.

She paused. "...What...?"

"It has been a year, Kathryn, and I have seen you eyeing me...because I've been eyeing you, as well."

"But why would you…tell me this…?"

"I would not have noticed your interest if I, myself, were not interested."

"Brother—"

"*Kathryn*," I said. "Do you mean to tell me that I am truly only a brother to you?"

"But isn't that how it should be? Your brother and I…I was his wife! W-we were intimate! He was my lawful husband, and I—"

"Kathryn," I said, interrupting her. "I know."

"…You know what?" She asked, wariness on her face.

"I already know about the circumstances between you and my brother."

She paused. "I don't know what you mean."

I chuckled and gave a sigh. "Kathryn, I know that you and Kenneth…only shared your wedding night."

She gaped at me. "…What…?"

"You are using your fear of the unknown to omit part of the truth, are you not?"

"I—"

"You and I both know that you and my brother were never intimate beyond that point, so tell me…were you even truly his wife, even in body? In legality's sake, yes, and technically, yes…but you weren't in love. You only slept together once, and only because of force of circumstances. Never did you choose to take his body inside of your own."

Her cheeks turned bright pink, her ears the same as her blush overtook her whole face. "I…I…even so, we can't do this—"

I sighed, even as I noticed the fear in her eyes when I took a pace back, letting go of her.

She gaped at me, confused.

"Very well, then. If I have misinterpreted your gaze and your blushes—if I have, truly, misunderstood your body language—then I ask that you forgive me."

She flinched, grabbing my sleeve to keep me from leaving. "Forgive you...?"

I nodded. "If you aren't ready to let go of my brother, then, please, continue to mourn him if you feel the need to. Ignore your feelings and mine, and continue to stay wallowing in your 'grief,'" I told her. "And I will not bother you with my feelings for you again, if that is what you wish. I can ignore my heart if that is what you demand of me."

She sputtered, clutching a hand over her heart. "Brother, I...K...Killian," she gasped out, tears running down her face, and I glanced at her sideways, giving her my attention.

I needed to make her come to me, on her own.

I couldn't push my feelings on her and expect her to just follow along.

She had to choose me of her own volition.

She hesitated, looking anywhere but me. "Killian, I..." She glanced at me, then away again...and I nodded, turning away from her.

"Take some more time to think, Kathryn. I will wait for you to come to a conclusion on your own," I smiled back at her, before I made my way to my horse, mounting and riding on back toward the manor.

We had ridden on horseback to get here, and so she would be fine to ride with Aaron on her way back home.

A couple of hours passed, and I reached the estate. I unmounted my horse and led him to the stable before I strode into my home, getting changed and into the bath that the maids had already prepared when I had arrived.

I stepped into the steaming water, sighing in relief as the heat melted over my aching muscles.

If she rejected me...I would respect her wishes, and I would no longer pursue her.

This was, after all, a gambit as it were.

Feelings or not, there was no guarantee that she would grant me permission to pursue her in earnest, and it wouldn't be "appropriate" for me to be with her to begin with...but to continue to pursue her hand after having already been rejected?

That would be very against code.

Within another thirty minutes, I heard the maids outside of my chambers, preparing and running a bath for Kathryn and letting her into the manor and to her chambers.

I stepped out of my bath, drying and dressing myself, leaving my body wrapped in a bath-robe and slipping some bedroom slippers onto my feet, wrapping the towel loosely around my shoulders to catch the droplets that fell from my hair.

I had a feeling...

About twenty more minutes later, I heard the door click down the hall, and I felt her approaching outside of my door, pausing when she had come to *my* door in particular, before she let out a breath softly...and, quietly, she knocked twice.

I stepped over to answer the door, taking note of her disheveled appearance and wet hair.

She cleared her throat. "May I...come in?" She asked, and I nodded, stepping to the side and out of her way.

I was surprised that she had taken the initiative to show up here, to my chambers. If anyone saw her or found out that she was here, freshly bathed, looking her current state...all manner of rumors and gossip would ensue.

It would make the current gossip look like a joke...

I let her into my chambers, and she stood close to me, facing the opposite direction.

• • •

"I must be honest with you...I think a great deal about you, Lord Killian. You are handsome and kind, caring and giving, with beautiful eyes and hair. Any woman would find you a very handsome man...but I...I don't understand, my lord, why you would take interest in *me*."

I gaped at her, shocked. "What?"

She looked up at me. "My question to you is this; *why* do you like me? Why do you want to be with me?" She threw her hands up, exasperated. "Furthermore, why did you ever even allow me to move into the manor? I know that your parents didn't agree with the decision! Even now, they push you to hold my social debut and being hosting meetings for me to interact with other young lords. So, I don't understand..."

I looked away for a moment, before I looked to her. "The truth?" I asked, and she nodded. "I originally felt empathetic toward you, because you were married to my brother against your will, and so much happened after that. I felt empathy toward you after the...after the fire," I said, clearing my throat. "Because I had lost my brother, and you had lost a husband. At first, it was completely innocent, I swear."

"But...?"

"*But*, the more time that you spent here, the more that I saw you...the more that I saw your smile, the small things that would make you laugh and watching your eyes twinkle...when you arrived, you were so timid and frightened, wary of kindness, seemingly afraid of me and my servants. However, as time passed, I watched you open up to us, and you blossomed."

"...Really?"

I nodded. "When we went to the Nivis Solstice banquet, I found myself seeing a *woman*, rather than a girl I felt brotherly towards. I began to find myself wondering if you were close to my brother, if you two had felt for one another the way that I felt for you. I wondered...did you look at him the way that you were beginning to look at me?"

She gasped, looking at me with new eyes, an awed expression on her face. "You..."

I stepped toward her, bringing her into my arms. "I would like the chance to make you mine...to become your *lover*, rather than a brother. If you aren't ready for that, or it hasn't been long enough since my brother's death for you...I will respect your wishes. I will honor that."

I could see the hesitation there, and I watched the emotions play over her face.

"May I...have a few days, to contemplate this, brother?" She asked me, and I almost cringed at the name she called me.

I sighed, but nodded. "If you promise me something in return."

"Yes?"

I met her eyes, leveling her with a heated, intense smoldering gaze. She trembled in my arms. "Please...do not call me 'brother' again, unless *that* it all that you are willing for me to be to you."

She gasped, meeting my gaze with surprised eyes.

"Let *that* be your answer, when you are coming to give me your conclusion."

She nodded, and I stroked her hair, scalp to ends, kissing the bundle of strands before I let it slide through my fingers, and I turned.

"Go on back to your chambers. You can find me again, when you have the answer."

She glanced back over her shoulder at me as she turned, before she stepped out of the room, and I shut my doors behind her.

The following morning, Aaron met me in my office.

"So...she asked for some more time?" He asked, and I nodded.

"She told you about it?" I asked. He stunned me even more when, right away, he nodded. "How long *has* she been talking to you about it?"

He chuckled. "Since Nivis's End."

"*What?*" I asked, shocked.

"She has been wondering about your behavior since you started having feelings for her. You haven't exactly been subtle, my lord."

I startled. "I...hadn't realized it had been that obvious."

He chuckled again. "It wasn't, to her. Initially, she thought that you were *angry* at her."

"Angry?" I asked, surprised. "What an absurd notion. Angry at myself, perhaps, for feeling that way for her and complicating things."

He smiled. "It wasn't until she questioned me about your responses that I told her that it was more of a romantic nature than anything else."

I smiled. "She didn't realize on her own?"

"Well," he hesitated. "She is only a sixteen-year-old girl," he reminded me. "And, to be honest, her experience with Lord Kenneth was extremely limited and..."

He hesitated long enough that it started to alarm me.

"And?"

"Traumatizing. She was upset the entire time, because nobody had taught her anything about lovemaking whatsoever. She had no idea what to expect. Lord Killian equated it to rape, himself."

"*What?*" I asked, horrified. "So...a girl raised as a lady, wasn't taught anything about the first night? Even after they told her about the arranged marriage? What is wrong with these people?" I asked, baffled. "You had informed me that they hadn't been as close as I might have thought, and that they only had their first night...but you didn't go into specifics like that. Good heavens..."

"That is precisely *why* she didn't come out of her room for the entire next month," he told me.

I sighed, saddened by this. "I had been wondering...That is heartbreaking." I glanced away. "Then...would she ever even be *capable* of having a normal relationship?"

He smiled. "If she was into the act herself, I don't think that she would be opposed."

I sighed, crossing my arms. "I wonder how long I will have to wait for her to give me an answer."

He glanced at me again. "She was quite flushed this morning, stroking her hair, and holding her hand over her heart. She told me her heartbeat was quite fast. I don't think it will take long."

I smiled, thinking about the conversation.

Chapter 12

Kathryn...

Veras's End, 1317 Imperial Lunar Year

It had been two weeks since I had gone to Killian's room in the night, and he had told me that he had feelings for me, that he wanted a chance to become my lover...

I couldn't see much reason to refuse, if I was being honest with myself.

Illegitimate or not, I was still the daughter of a marquess, and the wife of a marquess...and, I was *widowed*.

It was obvious that he didn't care if we had been in-laws. He seemed to be genuinely interested in pursuing me, no matter who liked it or didn't. I had to respect his sincerity and his determination.

Would I find any other nobleman willing to pursue me, if they found out that I was an illegitimate child?

I doubted it.

I knew that Killian was aware of the truth, and yet...it didn't change his mind.

I didn't want to be alone forever, and I did want for Carson to have a father...even if it were only a father-figure.

"Have you made a decision, my lady?" Aaron asked, doing my hair one morning.

"Well..." I sighed. "I have a question."

"Go ahead, my lady."

"What would happen...if I *don't* accept his request to start courting?"

He looked away; a bit hesitant. "As your current legal guardian—since your parents have given up their rights to your affairs but you aren't yet a legal adult—Lord Killian would be charged with hosting your social debut and putting you back on the marriage market, as that would be the next step in your social life."

I gaped at him, shock and fear spearing through me. "M-marriage market...? Not just a social debut? I thought he was only planning my social debut, but I was free to court other men if I chose to! You mean they are planning on putting me on the marriage market?"

He looked at me, surprised. "My lady?"

"So, he would just...just sell me off, just like that?"

"No! *No*, my lady, it wouldn't be like last time. No, Lord Killian would be sitting and interviewing the men with you, and supervising your courting...or, rather, having me to do so, as it would be very awkward for him to do that now that he has expressed his feelings for you."

I glanced at him. "And...what would happen if I *did* choose to accept his confession?"

He smiled. "Well, for one, I believe you would be much happier. Then the two of you would start courting, and if the two of you are happy together and have mutual feelings, then the two of you would marry and start a life together."

I gulped, thinking about this. "Would we...have to do the same thing that the marquess and I did, on our first night?" I asked, trembling.

"Oh, marchioness," my butler said, consoling me.

"I know it sounds silly, but—"

"It wouldn't be painful this time, and you would only do what you like and are comfortable with. Believe me, it wouldn't be something that you had to do. It would be something that, if you don't mind my saying so...you would come to want to do."

"Want...to do..." I let the phrase graze over my own tongue, testing it.

"My question for you, Marchioness...what is it that *you* wish for?"

I blushed. "I...I am not sure. I am so scared and confused, that I just...I don't know..."

"May I ask you a simpler question, then?" He asked, and I nodded. "How does the young lord *make you feel?* How do you feel when you look at him, and when he looks at you? How do you feel in his presence? When you even think of him?"

My heart began to beat much faster, and I gasped, gulping, and trying to catch my breath, my face heating rapidly. He chuckled, and pulled me into a light embrace, patting my back before he pulled away, and grabbed something off of my vanity, handing it to me.

I took the hand-held mirror from him, looking at myself and taking in my flushed face, the sweat beading on my forehead, the rapid pounding of my heart.

"*That*, my marchioness...*that* is your answer."

I glanced up at him. "But...isn't that...wrong?" I asked.

He shrugged. "Why would it be?"

"But...he's my brother by law."

"And?" He asked, unconcerned. "Marchioness, you were widowed. You could hardly even call what you had with Kenneth a marriage, in any case. There have been worse, closer, blood-related arrangements in society before. You two are not related by blood."

"Yes, but—"

"Had you and the marquess been particularly close, it may be a bit different, but the two of you were not, madam. The two of you...only had relations once. You have no reason to fret over such things."

I sighed, giving a nod. "But...wouldn't he be looked down upon, for being with me?"

"My dear marchioness...he is the heir to the Jayce duchy. He is in no way incapable of protecting himself. He is a skilled knight and a very well-educated young man. He would be a valuable asset to you, and to young master Carson."

I considered this. "Then...tell Lord Killian that I will meet him out at the gazebo tonight, to tell him my answer. I think we could have a nice walk around the gardens together. Oh, and...send in the maids."

He grinned at me, knowing what my answer would be from that statement alone.

I only asked for the *maids*, in plural, when I wanted to get dressed up.

A single maid would be more than sufficient for any chores I may need taken care of.

A group of maids was only needed in the case that I needed to be *dressed up*.

He stepped out, and I glanced at myself in the mirror again, cheeks still deep, rosy pink and my skin balmy, I was so nervous.

This was it. I had been at this estate for seven months, and Killian and I had...grown feelings for one another in that time.

The maids poured into the room, excited, as I told them what outfit that I wanted to wear and how I wanted to be dressed. They set to work, and as I snacked on some salad and light pastries, I watched them work around me like a whirlwind.

It took about three hours, but finally, the sun was starting to set and I took a good, long look at myself in the mirror to take in the maids' hard work.

"I...I look stunning," I whispered, taking it in.

I wore the floor-length sundress that Killian had gotten me for Nivis Solstice, and all of the accessories with it. My face was done with light powder and eyeliner, and a pretty pink lipstick shined on my lips.

The purples and lavenders against my skin-tone were pretty, and my hair was done up in a swept bun, falling into a curling spiral and spilling down to rest on my shoulder.

"You ladies have outdone yourselves," I smiled, looking at myself. I looked like a beautiful young lady out on the town, ready to meet prospective suitors...

In a way, I supposed that I *was* meeting a suitor.

A suitor that I had never anticipated.

One of the maids glanced out the window, and told me that Killian was on his way out, headed towards the gazebo at the back of the estate, through the gardens and near the ponds and fountain.

It was the most beautiful place on the estate.

Once he was out of sight, I took a deep breath, letting my maids lead me out of the room and out of the manor, do the steps and to the lawn.

Aaron turned, and he gasped when he saw me, kneeling by me.

"Marchioness," he whispered. "You look...ravishing."

I blushed. "Thank you, Aaron."

He smiled, standing, and holding out his arm for me, and I took it to let him escort me out to the gazebo.

It was about a fifteen-minute walk through the garden to the gazebo, but I didn't mind that. My shoes were comfortable, and my heart was racing too fast at what was happening to pay much mind to anything else.

When we got about five minutes from the gazebo, Aaron stopped.

"I will let you two have your privacy, and stay here. Continue along this path...and it will lead you to him," he said, soft.

The crickets were chirping and the lamp-posts had been lit along the path, so I smiled.

"Thank you, Aaron," I smiled, giving a small curtsy.

I continued onward, stepping lightly along the pathway, and as I came upon the gazebo, I could see Killian facing away from me and looking out over the small lake there.

I felt my heart thundering in my chest, wondering how he would react to what I was about to say.

I gulped, taking a deep, quiet breath...he still hadn't turned to face me.

Perhaps he didn't know I had come...

Perhaps he couldn't hear me; perhaps his heart was thundering in his ears just as loudly as my own heart thundered in mine. I felt like I would be sick, my heart was thumping so fast and my gut was clenching so hard.

I steadied myself, forcing myself not to feel faint.

I was brave. I could do this. I could do it. I had made my decision, I would be okay.

"...*Killian*," I spoke, soft, and he inhaled sharply, turning to face me.

His eyes spoke volumes before he could even take in my appearance, but then his eyes were taking me in and his own eyes widened, taken aback.

He stepped over to me, taking my hand gently. His other hand reached up to my cheek.

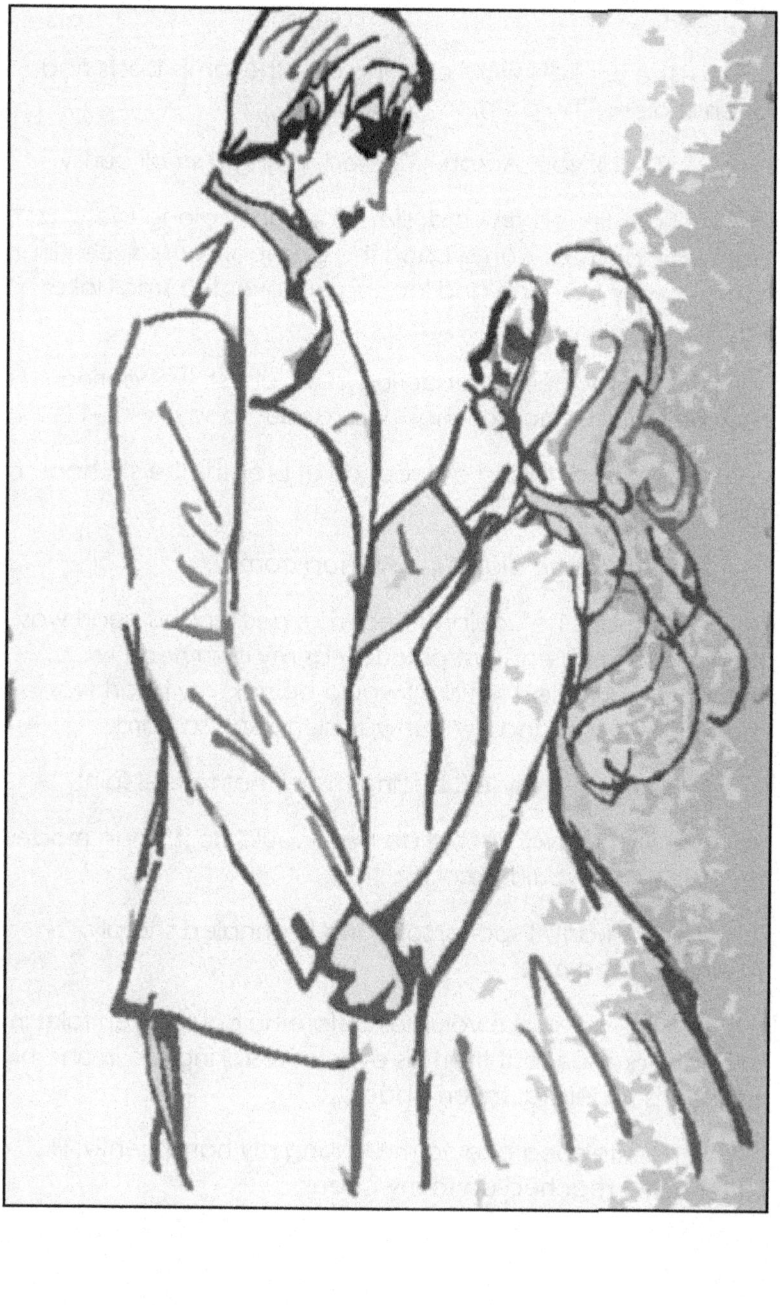

"*Kathryn,*" he whispered.

I smiled up at him. "I...I want to take this chance...with *you*," I said softly. "I accept your confession."

His eyes sparkled in the lamp light, and he very slowly—*more* than enough time for me to refuse him—took my face into his hands, holding me delicately and deliberately as if I would shatter into a million pieces.

He slowly leaned down, and pressed the gentlest of kisses to my lips.

He pulled away, seemingly taking my breath with him, and he smiled at me warmly as he took me by the hand, leading me to the bench nearby.

He took off his jacket, laying it on the wood and having me sit upon it before he sat beside of me, and he wrapped an arm around my shoulders.

I leaned into his side, resting my head on his shoulder even as we stared out over the lake, together.

I awoke sometime later, being carried in Killian's arms as we walked back to the estate.

"Hmm?" I asked, confused. "When...when did I fall asleep?"

He chuckled. "You fell asleep shortly after we sat down. You must have been quite tired. I am sorry to have exhausted you so, mentally, with all of these things to add to your mind."

I smiled. "No, it wasn't your fault. I just...haven't been sleeping well. I've been...worried."

"Worried?"

"Worried that you were angry at me for so long. At least, until Aaron explained your behavior."

He smiled. "I was only frustrated, because I felt that I shouldn't push my feelings onto you, in case you didn't feel the same. But I was too scared to ask you how you felt."

I smiled. "What matters, now, is that we are together...and that our feelings are mutual."

He smiled down at me. "Yes," he said, simply.

Chapter 13

Kathryn...

Folias's Blessing, 1317 Imperial Lunar Year

Both mine and Carson's birthdays had come and gone, and it was now a year since I had moved to the Jayce estate.

As time had passed, the servants had become *quite* aware of our growing closeness and our status as a couple.

By order of Killian, it was kept under lock and key on the estate, not allowed to be gossiped about, or else they looked at losing their jobs.

We hadn't shared more than three kisses, but we walked together around the gardens often, and held hands. He was very honorable and chivalrous with me, courteous and respectful at all times.

Now, it was coming upon the harvest time and the holidays yet again. I was growing nervous...because Killian had been speaking of going public with our relationship, and I wasn't sure how to proceed.

I enjoyed his company, and I cared for him.

We hadn't, however, come to say "I love you" to one another yet. If he was wanting to take things to a public level...didn't that mean that things were becoming *serious*?

As the prospect of others knowing of our relationship came to light, I wasn't sure how I felt about it. It thrilled me, but terrified me all at once.

How would other people respond?

I knew, from experience, that the maids and other servants had negative opinions about it, for the most part. They all glared at me when I was alone, and they gave us wary glances—if they looked at us at all—when we were together. Mainly, they tried to stay out of Killian's war path, as several members of staff had been fired for having...opinions that were "too loud."

The only person they didn't seem to look at negatively was my son, who had nothing to do with my personal relationship to his uncle.

That was another concern; how would *Carson* see Killian?

Would he stay his uncle?

Or would he become a father to Carson, and ask to be treated as his father?

It would need to be discussed soon, in reality, because Carson was already two years old...soon, however we told him to see Killian would be how he would see him from that point forward.

I sighed, shutting my book without even marking my page. I hadn't really been reading, anyway. I would have to try again later.

I looked at myself in the mirror, my concern etched into my face.

"What is the matter, marchioness?" He asked as he knocked on my open bedroom doors, stepping in. "Are you alright?"

"I've been thinking about what you said the other day," I said, smiling slightly. "I...I'm nervous to take our relationship public, Killian."

"Why?"

"Well, I...I feel like it must seem strange, after Kenneth's death."

He shrugged. "I'm not worried about that," he smiled, coming to take me in his arms, pressing a gentle kiss to my forehead. "I care for you a great deal, Kathryn...I want to make our relationship public, and take things with you to the next level. We have been courting for quite some time."

I smiled, feeling relieved. "I...I suppose it is time," I said. "I just...wanted to make sure that you were sure."

He laughed. "I am ready. Do you...want to stay with me?"

I nodded, blushing as I pressed my face to hide in his chest. He chuckled, hugging me in his arms and rocking me a little.

"Alright then," he said. "That is settled. We will make things public at this year's harvest festival. We missed it last year due to everything going on, remember? And the year before, you had your wedding that same week, so the two of you missed it then, as well."

He was right; I hadn't been to the harvest festival, a very popular, very public fair-like event that took place annually in Folias's Blessing.

As it happened, the event was only a few days away, and trepidation struck through me. That wasn't much time to prepare...

"I actually...bought you something, for the festival," he said, smiling. He turned, stepping back out of the door, bending to pick up something from behind the wall before he turned back and brought me a box. "I hope that you like it," he smiled.

I opened the box tied closed with a jade-green ribbon, and I gasped at the beautiful, modest-cut, deep green gown.

It had long sleeves and blouse-type top and bodice, tying in the back with a golden-tie, corset-style closing method.

The hips were seamed in so that the gown of the dress looked separate, almost, but it puffed out a bit, creating a bigger silhouette on the bottom.

There was gold and auburn-orange embroidery and trim-work all over the gown, with lace work in the same colors at the hems of the gown's train and sleeves, as well as around the neckline.

It looked like a true madam's gown, beautiful and elegant.

Along with the dress was a knitted gold and auburn shawl with some green threading along it, and a lady's small top-hat in a beautiful cream color with green leaves, a small pine cone and gold beading.

There was a pair of tan-colored boots with green and gold decorations sewn into the toes, golden lacework along the heels.

I gasped, taking in this gown. "It is lovely," I smiled brightly for him. "Thank you, Killian," I smiled.

He blushed slightly, smiling, and giving me a nod and a warm expression before he gave me a slight bow.

"I'll leave you for the evening, then. I will be busy with paperwork for the next few days in preparation to take the day of the festival off, so I probably won't see you much until then." He pressed a small kiss to my lips. "Good night, Kathryn."

"Good night, Killian," I smiled, watching him walk out of the room...

I caught myself staring at his firm, nice bottom, and I blushed heavily at myself.

"What in the world am I watching...?" I whispered to myself, shaking my head at how audacious that was.

I was ogling the poor thing, no better than a cat-caller I was.

Four days passed, and it was the day of the festival. True to what he had told me before, I hadn't seen Killian much over the next few days. He had missed his meals, and I had seen him pouring over stacks of papers in his office, diligent to get things done.

That morning, however, after breakfast, he came out dressed in a suit that had many similarities to my own outfit;

He wore a taupe-colored suit with a green vest beneath the outer coat, gold embroidery all over the vest, and a cream-colored button-up shirt beneath the vest.

He wore taupe pants that were tucked into tan boots that had gold and green trim-work. He wore a taupe top-hat with a gold and green ribbon tied around it in the typical men's fashion.

I blushed, thinking of the implication...

In this society, if a man matched his outfit to a lady's and they were adults...it was a symbol that they were a couple.

It was blatantly stating their intention to court one another.

Couple's outfits had recently become popular in society, and they were each completely customized so that there weren't any copies out on the market...

That meant that he hadn't just gone and bought me any gown and accessories...he had specially ordered a custom-made gown and an outfit for himself to match.

I turned as the nanny brought out my son, and I gasped when I saw him. He looked dashing, like a little man, in his own suit.

He wore a taupe-colored coat and shorts, with a blue and silver vest that matched Marquess Soren's house colors. He wore tan boots with blue trim-work, and then I saw it;

Around his neck was a scarf of blue and green knitted together, representing both the marquess Soren and the duke Jayce households.

There was only one meaning behind such a thing; to match our outfits;

*Killian Jayce intended to propose **marriage**.*

Had it been under different circumstances, I wouldn't have thought so, but after he had custom-ordered couple's outfits and even a similar but different ensemble for Carson, the scarf definitely implied that conclusion.

I glanced to butler Aaron, confused, but his wide grin only confirmed my suspicions.

I turned my attention to the cars, where Killian was helping the maid load Carson inside, and then he turned to me, an almost-blinding smile on his face, his teeth perfect as he smiled.

It was hard to look at him, he was so perfect...how had this man shown interest in me in a romantic sense?

I was startled at my own thoughts.

When had I started thinking that he was perfect...?

He helped me up into the car, and we rode the hour journey that it took to reach the festival grounds.

The festival took place near the center of the fief, not far from the duke's estate.

We arrived, spectators gathering along the path to welcome us as we pulled up through the drive around, and as we stepped out and Killian paused at the door, holding his hand out to the car, I could hear the gossips and the newsies calling out that he was escorting a lady, asking if he had finally chosen a woman to settle with.

It was, according to our society's current tradition, a little late for him to be settling.

He would be twenty-one this coming Blizzard's Reign, and that was a bit late to be marrying in today's social economy...especially considering that, as he was hitting this new adulthood, he would be inheriting the duke's title officially.

Kenneth would have, at the age of twenty-one, been appointed as the marquess the following year, when he turned twenty-one. He had been two-and-a-half years older than I, and thus he would have been almost twenty, now...had he been alive, that is.

When I handed him my hand and stepped out of the car, reporters immediately flocked to us, bombarding us with questions...that is, until they saw who I actually was, and a collective gasp was heard throughout the crowd.

Despite having an intimate wedding with Kenneth, there had been reporters who had tried to get into the wedding, and reporters who had remarked on the union in the local papers. There had also been several reporters who had attempted to interview Kenneth at the Soren Manor, but to no avail.

When the fire had ravaged the mansion, it had been in the newspapers and spread across the nation, detailing that he had left behind a wife and son.

That wife being me.

Whispers and gossip ran rampant as soon as I pulled my son from the car, bringing him to rest on my hip, even as everyone stared and looked at us in shock.

"Lord Jayce, who is this woman?" One reporter shouted. "Is this to be your duchess?"

"Can we get the reason behind you bringing the marchioness?!" Another reporter asked in a shout from the crowd.

"The marchioness?" Others asked, who hadn't realized. "That's the *marchioness*?!"

"Are you and Marchioness Soren now seeing one another as a *couple*?!"

As the servants fought to clear a path for us against the crowd, more and more questions came. Murmurs and scolding glances, glares, snickers. Questions asking if this was the heir to the Soren Marquess title, if he was adopting my son, if we were getting married...

It wasn't until *one* question, in particular, rung out through the empty air—as the rest of the reporters were taking a breath, almost, in a sudden hush—that made Killian freeze, and made my heart drop into my gut.

"Was the Marchioness Soren having an affair with you while Marquess Kenneth was still alive?! Is that why he was murdered!? Did she seduce you in order to raise her own standing?!"

I cried out in horror at the question, gaping at the journalist, who froze even as Killian paused, turning toward him with a frigid expression and cold eyes.

"What...did you just say?" He asked.

The crowd went silent, and as expected, the reporter refused to repeat his question.

Killian snarled. "You all want a comment? Jot *this* down in your notes, then; Upon the death of the Marquess and after overstaying her welcome at her parents' home, *I* reached out myself and *I* extended the invitation for Marchioness Soren to move into my estate, on the guise that I would become her guardian. Marchioness Soren and I, however, became quite close and she and I became romantically involved and started courting, since we were already good friends. She has accepted my request to take the relationship public, and we are hoping for further developments soon."

"Then—"

"Marchioness Soren was *not responsible*, in any way, for the terrible fire that claimed my brothers' and several others' lives! She herself, almost died in that fire. There are incident reports and medical records to prove as much. Now...I will not be answering any further questions."

He took my arm and led me through the crowd as they thronged and shouted and murmured, clamoring and chattering loudly, but we ignored them.

However, I couldn't hear anything.

I couldn't even see straight, as blackness blossomed behind my vision.

Murder...

I had just been accused of **adultery** and **murder**.

I had never once anticipated such a thing to be blamed on me, let alone thought by anyone. I had not once even thought that Kenneth could have been murdered, but the questions began pounding through my addled mind.

Had he been murdered?

Was it a murder case, and not just a fire?

Who stood to gain the most from his death? He certainly had political enemies, I was sure, but I hadn't ever been involved in any of his business or political dealings, so I had no idea.

Had he been involved in dangerous work?

Not to mention, accusing me of adultery?

Asking if I'd had an affair? If that affair was why my husband was killed?

They were implying that I killed my husband because I loved his brother...

I felt sick, and I quickly passed Carson off to a maid as the world around me spun.

I barely saw Killian's worried face as he called out for me, trying to catch me as I sank into the darkness.

When I awoke next, I was in a bed. I gasped, clutching my chest, looking around the room.

"Easy, my lady," butler Aaron said, quick to be at my side and assure me even as he held a cup of tea for me to sip on. "This tea has medicine in it, so it will help you rest."

I nodded, taking a sip. "What...what happened...?"

"You fainted, my lady...you fainted, and Lord Killian insisted that we return immediately."

"How long ago was that?"

"Two days."

Two days?

I had been unconscious for *two whole days?*

I suddenly felt water douse the flame of my embarrassment in my mind, as I heard shouts from down the hall.

"You cannot honestly be *serious!*" I heard the voice, and I startled to realize what was happening.

"His grace, Duke Jayce...he just saw the news, because he just read the newspapers." Aaron sighed, and that was all the explanation that I needed.

He was scolding Killian, then...for being with me.

"Can I...can I see the latest papers from the two days I have been out of it, Aaron?"

He cringed. "Are you...sure, my lady? I don't mean to question your choice, but it...it isn't pretty."

I nodded. "I need to know what's happening."

He gave a nod, and brought me three newspapers. One from the day after the incident, the following day, and one from this morning.

I opened the one from *today*, first.

The headline read:

"Reporters refused at the gates of the duke's estate; why hide, if there's nothing to hide?"

I cringed, but looked through to see photos of Killian glaring out of the windows at the reporters, before photos caught him shutting the curtains.

I sighed, opening the next newspaper from the previous day. The headline read:

"If they get married, how will the succession work? Is Duke Killian adopting his nephew?! How confusing!"

On the page were photos of my son, struggling in the maid's arms as they fled the scene.

"The first paper, from the day after the incident, has an entire page...not just a small section," Aaron said, cringing.

I took it gingerly, almost afraid...but I had to know.

I cringed when I saw the headline of *this* paper:

"Blooming Duke Jayce finally chooses his duchess—his SISTER?!"

The article showed photos of him helping me out of the car, and photos of me losing consciousness at the end of the incident.

I read on, taking in the article.

"*Just what is it about Lady Kathryn Abraham that sucks in the men of this family? As we all know, Kenneth Jayce—who became Marquess Kenneth Soren, succeeding his maternal grandfather's title—was wed to miss Abraham in the year 1314. We also know that within a month, the young girl was with child...though, questions to her child's true paternity are now in question, as only a year after the fire that claimed the life of her marquess, marchioness Soren moved in with another man—her husband's brother, blooming duke Killian Jayce!*

"*Lord Jayce is quoted as saying that he had taken her in with the intention to become her guardian and host her debut, as well as put her back on the market...but is that truly the case? I ask you, why was it so imperative to take in the wife of your brother just shortly after his death? Not only that, but to quickly enter into a personal, romantic relationship?*

"*Sources say the two began seeing one another romantically only a couple of months after the death of the marquess, so my question, as a curious reporter and responsible journalist...'were they in the middle of a love affair before the marquess died?' Furthermore, I question: 'Did their love affair strike the desire to kill the marquess, resulting in the fire that completely destroyed the estate?'*

"*Lord Killian says that the marchioness was injured in the incident, and medical reports state that this is fact...but it is also fact that she fled the estate immediately after, and furthermore, when she received the insurance payment, she did not do her duty as the marchioness to rebuild the Soren Mansion. Rather, the whereabouts and use of that money is completely unknown.*

"How audacious it was, for the widowed marchioness to not only move in with her brother, but to arrive to a public venue in couples' clothing with the blooming duke!

"Lord Killian and the marchioness wore matching outfits, with young master Carson Soren in a similar ensemble, but the boy wore a particularly notable scarf along with his outfit beside of their matching attire; a scarf that sported the color of both houses.

"I leave it to the good judgment of our readers: do we really want our duchess to be a woman who is already widowed? For that matter, a woman who is the legal sister of our duke? It doesn't seem entirely right, to me, but that is simply this author's humble opinion. I'll probably lose my job for saying so.

"This raises so many questions, in the first place, but those can be answered later. All we can do now, is pray, pray, pray!"

Tears ran down my face as I finished reading the article, sobs bubbling out of my throat as I heard the shouting continue down the hall.

I had messed up.

I had completely, utterly made a mistake.

I should have never entered into a relationship with him…

I could no longer be romantically involved with Killian Jayce…even if that meant that I had to leave his estate, entirely.

I couldn't make my love, my first love…suffer because of me.

Chapter 14

Killian...

Veras's End, 1317 Imperial Lunar Year

I stood at the gazebo, waiting. She had asked the maids to have me wait for her at this place, saying that she would give me her answer.

I waited, and waited.

I barely heard a step as she approached—she was quite light on her feet, it seemed, because I normally didn't have any trouble hearing someone approach me.

I clenched my eyes closed, waiting for her to address me.

I knew that her response would determine our relationship moving forward; whether she chose to reject me, or to accept me, I would respect either wish.

I didn't actually *expect* her to accept me...I figured that she would turn down my offer, actually, wishing to stay the marchioness.

My entire world paused, when, against my expectations...

"*Killian*," she said, soft, and I startled.

Had she...truly just accepted me?

She told me that she wanted to take the chance with me, to become a couple, and my heart thumped wildly in my chest.

I was positively elated.

Solaris's Reign, 1317 SLY

Carson's second birthday had arrived, and we celebrated with a small party at the mansion.

It was simple and intimate, passing without a big fuss.

Kathryn's brother, Luther, had come to the mansion to celebrate with us, and he brought a nice gift for Carson as well; a toy rocking-horse.

He took the time to remind me—as if I had forgotten—that Kathryn's birthday was coming in Moon's Dance.

I had already decided on what to get for her.

I was giving her a horse.

She had mentioned that she loved my horses, and loved riding in general, so I was taking her to a stable a few hours away to choose a horse of her very own, to bring with us back to the estate and to keep here exclusively for her.

I was excited, as I had already made reservations and asked for them to prepare their finest mares for her.

Carson, in the meantime, was running around like a little wild-man, blazing through the manor and all of the toys like a forest fire. He had high energy, much as I remembered my brother had also had at that age. Seeing the boy, remembering what his father was like...it made me realize just how much he favored his father.

He may have gotten his mother's eyes, but he had gotten my brother's hair and face, certainly.

The same nose and ears, the same sandy hair, the same bone-structure...

It was crazy, how genetics worked. Despite looking so much like my brother, he had his mother's striking, violet-blue eyes that looked like a deep purple rather than a blue, but still counted as a blue all the same.

Those eyes that were so contrasting to mine and my brother's bright, golden green gazes.

It got me to thinking about the marchioness, herself.

She had those eyes, but her father didn't. Had they...been from her mother?

The maid who had given birth to Kathryn, I had discovered, no longer worked for the marquess. In fact, she had disappeared shortly after he had taken Kathryn from her, and she had never been heard from again. Whether she had gone into hiding or had been killed, I would likely never know.

Then, my mind wandered off to another question...

If Kathryn and I were to marry, and have children...what would they look like?

I shook myself from the question. We were still moving so slowly, so quietly...thinking about having children was a giant leap forward, even considering the possibility seemed like a far-off notion.

I didn't know when Kathryn would be ready for that, or if she ever even would be, for that matter.

We hadn't discussed it.

She was so cautious, so wary of opening up and getting closer, that we were moving at a snail's pace. I had to wait for the onion to peel back one thin layer at a time, and it was taking its time, for sure.

Moon's Dance, 1317 ILY

"You're...gifting me a horse?" Kathryn asked, eyes wide as pulled her hands away from her eyes at my instruction and taking in the view.

I nodded. "You mentioned how much you loved riding, so...here we are," I smiled.

She was in awe, taking in the line of horses that the ranch-hands had prepared, and she took an apple from the basket nearby.

She approached a horse, but all of the horses seemed...almost wary of her.

She stepped back, concerned...before she gasped, almost as if she sensed something, and turned the other direction.

I glanced back, taking notice of what she had her attention caught by.

All of the ranch hands warned her, trying to get her away even as she approached the horse and he approached her.

It was a young stallion, still in his youth before hitting his prime, but he was still quite large for his age.

He was a brilliant bronze-shade of brown, with midnight-black legs and hooves, and midnight-black mane and tail. His eyes were a bright, lustrous golden-brown.

He was a magnificent steed, certainly, but as he raised on his hindlegs, I startled, rushing to get her away—

Then, surprising us all, he hopped on his hindlegs and bucked, before coming back to normal.

Suddenly, he was nudging her playfully with his head, snatching the apple from her hands and rubbing into her, almost knocking her over.

She laughed and giggled.

"Th-that...I cannot believe it!" The headman of the ranch said. "We've been trying to break that boy ever since he arrived, two months ago! But absolutely nothing has worked. He must have taken a real shinin' to your wife, my lord."

"Oh, she...she isn't my wife," I said, soft. Disappointed.

I knew that I wanted to marry her, though...and soon.

"Oh, I do beg your pardon, sir," he said. "She is a lucky lady; he will be an excellent stallion when he matures a bit more. I can't believe what I saw!"

The other men came and chattered to him, and I went to Kathryn's side even as the stallion huffed and tried to shew me away with his head.

She laughed and pushed him back, scolding tone in her voice, and he immediately acquiesced to her.

"It is rather hard to believe that he hasn't even been broken in, yet."

"What?" She asked, stunned. "So...he's still wild!"

I nodded. "Only arrived two months ago."

"That's...*goodness*, I don't know what to say."

"That's why the mares were wary of him. He was coming to approach you, but many wild stallions try to dominate the mares of ranches when they arrive if they aren't separated," I said. "Wild mares are a bit more difficult to woo, I imagine," I laughed.

"So, which am I?" She asked, and I felt a frog leap up in my throat.

"What?" I choked.

"Am I a *ranch* mare, or a *wild* mare?"

I considered this, wanting to give her my honest opinion. "I think of you as a wild mare," I told her. "You have always wished to follow your own wishes, away from what was expected of you. You want to be a free spirit..."

She smiled. "But aren't wild mares harder to woo?"

"It just takes the right *stallion*," I said, suggestive, and she blushed heavily at the implication.

Folias's Blessing, 1317 ILY

In the aftermath of the incident at the festival, my father had come right away to give me a proper scolding for even *thinking* to *imagine* a romantic relationship with Kathryn...

Though, he had been equally surprised to learn that she *reciprocated* my feelings.

"Son, it just isn't proper. It isn't right for you, as her brother-in-law, to be with her romantically. I mean, for heaven's sake, she was bedded by your late brother!" He cried, hysterical. "He was *inside* of her; he gave her his seed and she bore him a child! Does that not...does that not *bother* you, in *any* fashion?" He asked, cringing for a moment as if a spider had crawled on his leg.

"Father, please," I said. "You are overreacting."

"Have you even *seen* what the news is reporting? They accuse her of having an affair! Is that true?"

"Of course not!" I cried, appalled. "Let me guess; you're also wondering if she murdered my brother?"

He paused, quiet, and I gasped.

"You mean...you *actually wonder*?"

"Well, how else could a fire start, in his room, without him noticing in the middle of the night? How else could he stayed in bed the entire ordeal, without even getting up? All of the evidence points to him already being dead in bed, before the fire even started!"

"W...what?" I asked, horrified. "When did *that* become a development? Who is your source? Why haven't I been informed?!" I cried.

"I hired a detective to look into the case, personally. He has been quite thorough, thus far."

"But father, Kathryn was with Carson in her chambers on the complete *opposite* side of the mansion. Even if he had, *somehow*, been killed in his bed without even waking up or struggling, how could she have gone to his chambers, lit the fire, and gone back to her chambers long enough for the blaze to heat the knob of her door where it burned and permanently imprinted and embedded the shape of the knob in her palm? There were witnesses who placed her in her room at the time of the blaze's worst point, and she was trapped with Carson in her room. It took Aaron going and busting the door down for them to be collected and taken to safety. If she had started the fire, don't you think she would have grabbed Carson and fled the estate immediately?"

"Only if she wanted to prove herself innocent that badly."

"Father!" I shouted. "You are acting like she is a criminal, when she is *family*! You cannot tell me that she intentionally almost died, just to try to prove her own innocence. You have lost your mind."

"No, *you* have lost *your* mind, boy," he told me, crossing his arms. "You cannot be thinking straight...and to think that you are inheriting the title of duke in only a mere two months!" He cried, upset.

"Why am *I* not thinking straight? Because I fell in love?! She was set into an arranged marriage with my brother. She was then widowed. And, so, what? I shouldn't be attracted to her or desire her for myself even over a year after his passing? I never saw her as a sister! She wasn't even part of the family for that long. What is so wrong about it? She doesn't even share my last name, but that of my grandfather."

"I don't wish you to be in a romantic relationship with someone who already has ties to our family that way! Think of her, son...the press is labeling her an adulteress, possibly a murderer...what will people say if you take her as your bride?"

"Why should I care?!"

My father stood there, silent for a moment, before he sighed, turning away. "Prove her innocence, first. Prove to me, without a shadow of a doubt, that she did not murder my son...and I will never make another objection to your relationship."

"I held out my hand and took his in a firm handshake. "Deal. And I will hold you to that."

My father sighed, looking away. "I already regret it."

My father finally took his leave, and I sighed, rubbing my head as I stepped out and went down the hall to Kathryn's room...

Only to startle, alarmed, as I found her packing a suitcase.

"What...*what are you doing?*" I asked, blood draining from my face.

She flinched. "I'm...going away."

"What?" I asked. "Kathryn, please—"

"'Marchioness,' 'Lady Soren,' or 'sister,' are the names you should refer to me as, brother."

Fearful rage struck me. "Are we *really* back to that? Kath—"

She held up her hand. "Lord Jayce. It isn't...it isn't appropriate. Our relationship isn't appropriate. I have caused you more than enough trouble, and I think it is time for me to go."

"No!" I cried, tears filling my eyes. "If you...if you cannot be with me in a relationship, at least allow me to continue hosting you in my estate. At least until you procure the means to move."

"But I—"

"Once your brother inherits the Marquess title, you will receive a sizeable amount of funds and you will be able to build the Marquess Soren estate once more. Please...stay until then."

She considered this. "Well...it is true that I have nowhere else to go."

"Exactly!" I said. "Please. I won't do anything that you aren't comfortable with."

She looked away. "I suppose that I will stay until I can get on my feet, then," she said, clearly upset.

"Kathryn...please. I don't want you to do this, and I know you don't want to do this. Kathryn, I...*I love you*," I told her, and she startled, looking at me.

Chapter 15

Killian...

"You...*love* me?"

I nodded, taking her into my arms. "Truly. I love you, Kathryn. I don't want for things to end like this."

"You can't...you *can't*...!"

"I can't?"

"You can't...do this to me!" She sobbed. "You can't, not when I already hardened my resolve!"

"I don't want you to leave, Kathryn," I repeated. "I love you. Please...I don't want you to leave me."

Tears filled her eyes. "I don't either. I...I love you, too, Killian. But this just...it can't work."

I brought my lips to press to hers, brushing against her own as I spoke. "Why can't it...?"

She turned away from me, still in my arms. "People will *always* judge us; they will never respect you if you take me as a wife, Killian. We will never be *free* to love one another."

I took in her words, and despite rationally knowing that she was right...in my heart, I couldn't accept it.

"*I don't care,*" I told her, kneeling before her, and pulling out a ring. "I...I had wanted to do this at another time, in a more romantic way, but...Kathryn, I want to spend the rest of my life as your husband. I want for you to marry me. You just admitted that you loved me, and I love you...can that not be enough?" I asked, begging her with my eyes to accept me.

"Lord Killian," she said, trembling.

"Kathryn..."

She didn't say anything further...she only dropped to her knees, taking me into her arms and bringing her lips to my own in an impassioned kiss.

I lifted her so that we stood, and I pulled her up so that her legs wrapped around my torso.

I carried her to my bed, and I lay her there, pressing kisses into her cheeks and upon her throat and collarbone.

I sat her on my lap, giving myself better access to her.

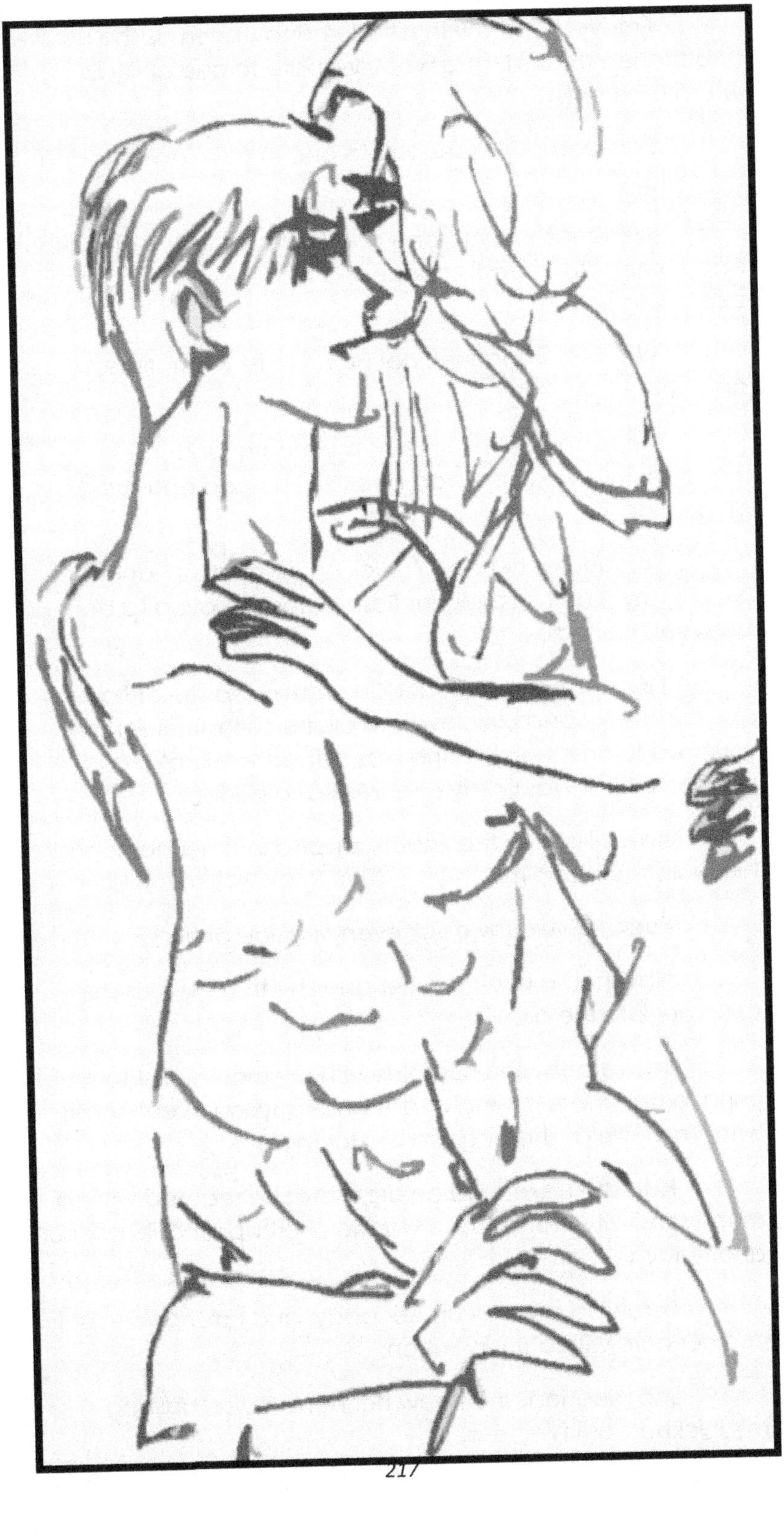

I moved deftly with nimble hands, even as she quickly unbuttoned my shirt, and we were bare to one another within moments.

I gasped out as she licked one of my nipples, loving her initiative.

We breathed into one another even as we clung to each other. Our breaths meshed, and we were so close to becoming one.

We were impatient, not wanting to waste time on decorum.

I took one of her tips into my mouth, and she moaned, throwing her head back as I nipped and sucked on her, moving down quickly.

I nipped at her naval, sucking on her torso and leaving my marks all over her flesh before I moved to be between her legs.

I liked the shape of her. She reminded me of flowers, soft and pretty and pink, even as cliché as that must have sounded to anyone else. She was soft and delicate, and so...so...pink. It was pretty and fresh and perfect.

It was tight on the finger I dipped into her heat, and her walls squeezed me.

Fuck...would my cock even fit inside of her?

I lavished a lick upon her and she trembled as she cried out into the air.

I dove between her folds with my mouth and tongue, using force, and felt her giving in and toppling over her cliff within minutes as she begged me for mercy.

Had she never had an orgasm? She reacted with so much sensitivity that I had to wonder. Perhaps I could ask her another time...

I crawled my way up her body, and I plunged myself into her core with a shaky moan.

She moaned and threw her head back, basking in my thickness as I filled her.

"I-I didn't know it could feel so good," she whined. "It's so good! So, so good," she ground her hips upward into me, thrusting up.

We gave one another all that we had, in that moment, and the night drew on with wild passion and airy cries of ecstasy that I was sure echoed throughout the mansion.

Was there anyone in the estate who didn't know what was happening?

I had to wonder.

I made her orgasm two more times that night as my cock stroked in and out, in and out of her tight, wet perfection, before she began to come in and out of consciousness. I pushed into her so deep that soft cries left her lips with no effort. My hands tingled as they stroked over her perfect tits and her tight ass, giving them loving squeezes, and she seemed to enjoy them, from the soft mewls she made.

"Good girl," I murmured. "Such a good girl. You feel so good, like heaven on my cock, wrapped around my body..."

Her hands gripped my hair, and then her nails dug into the skin of my back.

The sting was so fucking good...

I started to grind my dick deep inside of her, curving upward, hitting her internal g-spot, and she sobbed as her pussy began to weep, cumming wetly all over my rod.

"Fuck, what a good girl," I praised her. "Keep cumming for me, love. Keep sucking me deeper into you and soaking me with your juices."

She groaned, clutching her arms tighter around my neck and kissing my throat.

"I want to fill you up, baby. Is that okay? Can I fill your pretty pink pussy up with my cum? Can I shoot my load inside of you?"

She gasped, tightening, and clenching my cock as she came over me again, trembling.

"Y-yes," she whispered. "Yes, I-I want it. I want it," she begged.

"Oh, fuck, baby," I groaned. "I'm going to empty my cock inside you, that's what you want?"

She nodded fervently. "Yes," she confirmed, soft. "I want it, I want your cum!"

"*Fuck!*" I cried out.

I gave one last thrust, filling her to the brim with my release, and then pulled out to finish my drippings on her pale, creamy thighs.

I watched with a wild, heathenistic fascination as my thick, white cum slowly oozed out of her bright, swollen little pussy.

I almost came again, just looking at the sight, and more cum oozed out of my hole.

I got a wet cloth and cleaned her up lovingly as she drifted to sleep, a light snore coming up from her, and I chuckled at her as I watched her breathe for a few minutes. I cleaned her while she remained oblivious.

When I was finished, I pulled her so that she lay in my arms, I watched as tears streaked down her cheeks, even breaths through her nose as her chest rose and fell with her breaths.

I kissed her tears away, only praying that I could have her by my side forever.

I wasn't sure why she was crying, but I wanted to be there to wipe all of her tears away, listen to all of her worries and woes, watch over my nephew and any future children we may have…together, forever.

I wanted forever with this woman, and I knew it in my heart that I was truly done for.

I may have been older than her, and many men my age sewed their wild oats with women from towns and brothels to get experience...but I had not done so.

I was...or had been, only an hour ago, a virgin.

She'd had more experience than I.

I let a finger slip between her legs, feeling my essence slick there as it continuously dripped out of her core, and I felt myself harden again.

Would she get pregnant on our first night, as she had with my brother?

I couldn't bring myself to be regretful; if anything, I hoped so. I wouldn't be upset in the slightest if she became pregnant with my child.

This...was my forever girl.

I would make it happen, if she was willing. I would never force her, of course, but I couldn't help but want to monopolize her and make her mine.

If she got pregnant with my child...?

That would give her all the more reason to marry me.

A few more days passed by, and the news outlets continued pumping out articles about us, though they were getting low on grist.

Thankfully, I'd locked down the mansion, and nobody was talking about the newest state of mine and Kathryn's relationship.

It was obvious that she and I had made love, because we had been loud and obvious about it when it was taking place, but if by chance there had been anyone who *hadn't* known by the next morning, they certainly could tell when the maids found us together in one bed the next morning.

Most of the servants made it clear that they were happy for us, but there were a handful who didn't hide that they felt it was...not appropriate.

Who gave a fuck what they thought, though?

As long as they were paid well and did their jobs and didn't run their mouths, I didn't have a problem.

They had been the least of my concerns, however.

Reporters had just now, finally, stopped dropping by the mansion, taking our "no comment" and finally accepting that we wouldn't be giving any statements.

I was thankful.

I had not seen Kathryn look me in the eye since the night that I had proposed and we'd made love; she blushed heavily and looked away from me each time she saw me, and I could see her hand clench the fabric over her chest where her heart lay.

When we had been found the following morning, she had cried with flamed cheeks and hidden beneath the blankets until I had finally given her some privacy, and when I had returned to the room, she had been gone—taking a bath and avoiding eye-contact with me out of sheer embarrassment.

I could see her squeezing her legs together and crossing her legs around me, though, so I knew that being around me was having an effect on her.

I was glad.

She was embarrassed by how wanton she had been with me. It was seen as undignified in high society for a lady to be so...*blatantly sexual*, especially before marriage.

Full intercourse before marriage was practically a taboo in our society.

It was not that uncommon of a thing among commoner women, but among *noble ladies*, it was a frowned-upon behavior, that level of debauchery.

I blushed myself, remembering her writhing beneath me as she cried my name, gasping into the night air and breasts bouncing in time with my thrusts into her body. I felt my cock get hard.

I wanted her...

I wanted her again, already. She had left me like a man in the desert with nothing to drink;

I couldn't get enough of her.

A week passed by soon enough, and I was surprised when I received a report that I had been waiting for from someone in particular.

Luther Abraham had discovered, in his parents' vault, the receipt of my charge's insurance payment for the Soren mansion.

That was not all, however.

I had asked him to be keeping his eyes peeled for something else, as well, because we had kept my brother's letters to us.

It was the only evidence we'd had that something had been amiss between the Abraham family and my brother, as any other evidence from the marquessate had been effectively erased by the fire.

This one piece of evidence could change everything, and my heart raced in my chest as I looked at the words...the ink formed scribbles on this paper that told me, in all-but-an-admitted-verbal-confession, evidence of who was behind my brother's death.

His murder. He had been murdered.

This was the closest thing to proof I'd had so far.

It was a receipt that said "*Mission completed,*" with a sum of **ten-thousand gold pieces paid.**

The receipt was only signed with a bloody thumb print. Not even an initial.

This rose the question; what was the mission that had been completed?

Furthermore, *why, pray tell,* had that very slip of paper been filed along with the receipt of Marchioness Soren's *insurance payment that she never even received...?*

Was this the answer?

I could see nothing but red as I realized that this was the receipt from the assassin for his job, completed.

The ones behind the fire were who I had suspected, yet also feared...

My lover's parents.

Chapter 16

Kathryn...

I woke the morning after I had made love to Killian, my entire body boiling with my flaming embarrassment.

How had I been able to act so brazenly?

How shameful!

I had just resolved to myself to not be with him romantically just that day, and not even twenty-four hours had passed before I was taking him into my body, clutching to him despairingly like some...like some *bar-maid*!

It had been mind-blowing, yes. I was already throbbing, imagining him between my legs with his mouth and his tongue on me and his hard, stiff...

His cock inside of me...throbbing and pulsing hotly as he filled my insides with every drop he could give me, straight to my womb.

I trembled.

I had never known that it could feel this good.

I felt so incredibly guilty, realizing that this was what Kenneth had tried to do, but I had been so scared and alarmed and bitter...

He'd tried to make it good for me...

Killian, though...

His body...oh, how amazing his thick, muscular body had been on top of me, as he had pushed his thick, wide, angular hips into my own over, and over, and over again...

Those thick, powerful thighs...

That deep, thick, muscular "V" shape that led down to his manhood, and the thin trail of curly, dark, soft hair that trailed from around his belly button, down, and ended at the small patch of trimmed hair above his length...

How thick his length had been, filling me and leaving me breathless even as I clung to him for more, begging him...

I blushed as I felt my insides pulse and throb, begging and pleading to be filled again, standing quietly, and fleeing his room, wrapping my clothes around me without even putting them on and running through the hall to my chambers without even stopping to explain to butler Aaron, who stood and gaped at me in shock even as the maids who had come in was left sputtering after finding the scene.

How embarrassing!

I wasn't brave enough to face Killian directly or meet his eyes for almost two weeks after that night...but finally, he arrived on the sixteenth day, and knocked on my chamber door.

I opened it, blushing profusely as he stood there, clearing his throat, and holding out a letter to me.

"I am here for something serious," he told me, and I threw away my dirty gutter thoughts to pay attention to his words. "Your brother is about to succeed the Marquess Abraham title, and he invited you to the naming ceremony."

...I was stunned, beyond all imagining, that my parents had even allowed that piece of mail to leave the estate.

How big of a tantrum had Luther thrown over that, to get them to agree to him inviting me?

Or, was it because they had seen the news and knew that I was now romantically involved with Killian? Were they trying to save face with the duke's family?

I was just surprised that they allowed me to receive an invitation at all. I knew that they filtered and censored and blocked incoming and outgoing mail well enough.

"I see."

"I wanted to attend with you, if I may...as your betrothed. You never gave me an official 'yes,' but I would like to get an answer from you and attend with you," he grinned.

My cheeks flamed, and I looked away. "I-Is that a good idea? I feel like you shouldn't."

He came closer to me, leaning to whisper in my ear. "Do I vex you so?"

I blushed, feeling guilty. "Of course, not. I just...I feel that I need to attend alone. I will just damage your reputation. I should go to the event on my own, without someone else."

He glanced at me warily. "I am not convinced that is so," he said. "I believe that we need to stay united, now, in this time of uncertainty. The papers and high society already know of our intimate relationship, Kathryn. There is no point trying to hide it. In fact, me not going would only give rise to more whispers and rumors. You need for me to attend with you, to cement it into their minds that you and I are together."

"Well..."

"Besides...there is something that I wish to confirm, and an important matter that I must discuss with the new marquess. It is important for me to go." His face grew dark, and I startled, alarmed by the sheer coldness and sharpness of his gaze.

Why...why had he so suddenly shifted?

I didn't give any more protest.

I had a feeling that I would find out his true purpose at the event.

Year's Fall, 1317 ILY

Almost three weeks later, it was time for the naming ceremony for my brother, and Killian and I once again wore matching outfits to the event.

It was a statement to society.

When we arrived, we were welcomed much in the manner that I thought we would be; gaped at and whispered about, even as Killian took my hand in his and walked confidently with his head held high through the estate.

We made our way to my brother, and I dipped in curtsy as Killian nodded his head.

"Marquess...it is an honor to greet you by your newfound title."

"Thank you, Lord Killian." He glanced to me, then back to Killian, before he gave a bow. "I suppose that the rumors were not unfounded, after all. You look lovely, sister. It is truly joyous for me to see you looking so much better, and much healthier."

"Ah, yes," Killian said, tightening his hold on my arm a bit, gazing at me tenderly. "Though we know how it must look to outsiders...we simply couldn't hide our feelings for one another any longer. We fought against it for a while, but we finally decided to not care what society thought of us. I am happy with her."

"Hm," Luther said. "If my sister is happy, then I am happy for her. She didn't get much choice in her last marriage, so if this is her choice...then I support you both."

"Thank you."

"Take care of her, and I will wish you the very best from life. I will be rooting for you both. I hope it turns out better for her, this time around."

I gave another dip. "Thank you, brother," I blushed.

Luther leaned in a bit, but I barely heard what he whispered to Killian.

"I have already secured the funds for transfer, and have the check written out. I will send it over first thing in the morning, and if there are any other issues, do not even hesitate to contact me immediately. I want to make sure to right this situation."

What...were they talking about...?

Check?

"Thank you, Marquess," Killian said. "And the *other* matter...?"

Luther's face grew dark, and fear struck me. I had never seen his face so bleak.

What was happening?

He gave a slow, single nod.

"I see..." Killian glanced to me. "That is even more troublesome, then. Very worrying... If word got out—"

"My title, and Kathryn's standing, would fall to the wayside. We would be completely ruined. I have to admit, I...am at a loss for what to do, here."

I gaped at them. "Could someone please explain to me what is wrong?" I asked, and they glanced at me, before they ushered me out, and we stepped out to go to another room entirely.

"Sister," Luther addressed. "We...Lord Killian and I, I mean...we have found out the killers behind the death of Marquess Soren..."

I startled, horrified. "You mean...you mean he was, truly, murdered? That wasn't just a rumor? There was someone behind the fire?"

Luther nodded. "Not just the fire. After the fire, when Lord Kenneth's body was found...there were stab wounds found in the body, despite being found burnt almost past recognition. He was stabbed in the throat, with no time to react—"

I felt myself reeling, and I stumbled over to vase on the table holding a bouquet of flowers.

I dumped it, little care to the mess I made, and emptied the contents of my stomach into the vase with horrible, heaving wretches.

My husband was murdered.

They tried to murder Carson and I, too.

Oh, heavens. Oh, heavens! Heavens, have mercy!

Murdered.

Who was behind this—?

They glanced at each other before they watched me with sympathy.

"I know...this must be a lot to take in," Luther said. "But the fact is, your husband was not simply lost in a fire. He was killed, and your mansion was set afire. The assassin didn't need to kill you and Carson, however. He left you two alone. Then, Killian reached out to me a while back, asking me to look into this with him, to see if I could help him find the evidence. We have been struggling to find the culprits for a while, but then it struck us as odd."

"What did?" I asked, after wiping my mouth with the wet-wipe that butler Aaron handed to me, cleaning my mess as I focused my attention back to my brother and my lover.

"When you came to stay here, father and mother weren't nearly as angry as we had anticipated, were they? They weren't happy, of course, but they didn't make you leave. Why?"

I couldn't answer him. I just stared at him in numbed confusion.

"Furthermore, you didn't receive the compensation from the insurance on the mansion to be able to rebuild it, despite that *you*—and you alone—were the recipient of the check that arrived in the mail—the mail that had been being withheld from you. Why?"

The implications swirled around in my mind, and it hit me with dizzying force.

Was he saying that our parents...They took my...

They hired the...?

"Are...are you...are you saying that...?"

Killian nodded. "Yes. Your father and mother knew that the Soren mansion was insured in the event of a disaster. They calculated that if the manor burned to the ground, the insurance would come through to Kenneth, and he would rebuild the estate for its original worth. They were hassling Kenneth to repay what he owed for their support and financial backing, because they had their own agendas to see to."

"So...they...?"

Killian continued. "Kenneth showed me and our parents the threatening letters he had received, if you recall, and you remember that he had been forced into a car accident. The threats continued, and your parents couldn't get Kenneth to break. So, the plotted to set the mansion on fire, to get the insurance payout and make Kenneth go through a lot more trouble. But then, they something else crossed their minds: If Kenneth were unable to receive the payment because he died in the fire, then you—"

"Then *I* would be the next in line to receive the payment, if I survived." I put the dots together. "They knew that the payment would come to you."

Luther nodded. "That is why the assassin that was sent into the estate didn't come after you, nor Carson. Your lives were never the targets—it was the sizeable insurance payout that would be surely coming to you."

I felt sick again, and black spots formed behind my vision.

"I...I don't..."

"Father and mother sent an assassin to kill Marquess Soren in his sleep and set fire to the estate. They assumed that you and Carson—or Carson, at least—would survive the fire, thanks to the staff. The remaining members of house Soren would come to live back at the Abraham estate, of course. Then, they could control your mail received and sent out, they could go and cash the check for you—"

"*Stop!*" I sobbed, leaning on a desk nearby. "Please..."

"As the new Marquess Abraham," Luther said, in conclusion. "I am sending you a check for the exact amount of funds that our parents stole from you...for you to use however you see fit. It would be most proper, of course, for you to rebuild the Marquess Soren estate, and return with Carson."

"But I—"

"*However,*" he said, cutting me off. "If Lord Killian has declared his intentions with you, and you two plan to marry...then the estate will pass to Carson as soon as he comes of age, and any further children you have will be heirs to the duke's title rather than the marquess."

I glanced to Killian, who had a serious look on his face. "The question now, is...how do we proceed? They think that they have gotten away with it. They think that they weren't caught. How can we ruin them, without ruining the *entire* Abraham name, including you and your brother?"

"Well, to start off...I think it is time to raise my status so that they cannot ever look down upon me again," I said. I looked to Killian, who gaped at me, surprised, standing and unfolding his arms. "Killian—"

"Yes," he said, nodding. I looked at him, confused, so he elaborated. "I know you love me, but have been hesitating because of our circumstances."

"I—"

"I know that you are only suggesting this, *now*, in order to exact revenge...but yes. Let us marry, right away."

Luther glanced between us, shocked at this outcome. "That's your proposal?" He grinned, looking between us. "Alright, then. When will you marry?"

"There is a priest here, now, is there not? He performed the entitlement ceremony, right?"

Luther and I gaped at him. "You mean...you intend to marry *now*?" Luther asked, surprised.

Killian took my hands, looking at me with anticipating eyes. "If Marchioness Soren is willing," he smiled at me, and they both looked to me.

I thought it over in my head, quickly.

I wanted to get back at my parents and ruin them for what they had done. I wanted to raise my status so that they could never harm me or look down upon me again. I wanted to make them angry, to get beneath their skin. Besides loving Killian, he could assist me in doing that very thing at this very moment...

I nodded, a brilliant smile on my face. "Yes. I would like to marry you; now."

His face brightened immensely, and he glanced to Luther, who kneeled at our feet.

"It is my honor to host your pre-emptive wedding," he smiled up at us. "Congratulations, my sister." He stood, and we followed him as he strode out into the banquet hall again, attention falling to him as he gathered everyone's attention.

"Everyone!" He called. "I have an announcement to make. As of this afternoon, blooming duke Jayce has chosen his intended duchess, and made a formal proposal to her with my permission as her older brother and the head of the Marquess Abraham title; therefore, it is with great happiness that I hold the quick ceremony for their nuptials, here and now!"

Everyone gaped and gasped, murmurs and whispers flooding the space even as my parents gaped and gave deeply horrified expressions of anger, visibly upset and sputtering out irritated curses.

The priest quickly came to stand in front of us, in front of the crowd, and had us join hands even as my brother quickly murmured something into his ear. His eyes got wide, and he nodded. Then, he turned his attention to us, and had us look at each other.

"In the sight of God and men, do you, Lord Killian Jayce, take this woman, Marchioness Kathryn Soren, to be your lawfully wedded wife?"

"I do," he proclaimed, proud and steady.

"In the sight of God and men, do you, Marchioness Kathryn Soren, take this man, Lord Killian Jayce, to be your lawfully wedded husband?"

I glanced to my brother, who gave a smile and a nod, and then to my parents...who looked on in horror and screamed out to stop the wedding.

"I do," I said, smiling brightly to Killian.

"In the name of the Holy Trinity and in the name of his majesty the emperor, I hereby grant and name you as husband and wife, Duke and Duchess Jayce to be. You may kiss your bride, my lord," he said to Killian.

With a triumphant expression, Killian pulled me into his embrace and brought his lips eagerly to my own, kissing me passionately even in front of everyone.

"She must be pregnant," "He must have knocked her up! How horrible," "She must have seduced him to gain higher status, just as she seduced the young marquess. What a power-hungry villainess!"

We heard among the whispers, but I paid them no heed.

I was the future duchess, Marchioness Soren and Lady Jayce all in one.

I did feel powerful, as my status was surely climbing...and I ate up every moment of watching my parents spit out and sputter in rage, gaping and cursing me, rushing up to us to begin their tirade.

I was officially married to a man who would be Duke Jayce in just a couple of months, and I was officially out from beneath their thumb.

My power now exceeded their own.

I was under their skin.

Let's do this!

Chapter 17

Killian...

Year's Fall, 1317 Imperial Lunar Year

There had been a complete uproar as Kathryn's father and his wife had thrown a fit after our marriage. I expected that I would be getting an earful from my parents, as well, but it was too late;

Kathryn was my legal wife, now.

She had stood her ground, there in front of her parents, who proudly disowned her from the Abraham Marquessate family for bringing such shame upon them...but she had remained completely unbothered, and they had been even angrier at her lack of care about their decision.

My parents promised to discuss the situation with me later, but there wasn't anything that they could do to change it, now.

We made the journey back to the estate, kissing and groping on the train all the way as we traveled, as I took in her taste and smell; I could hardly wait to get back to the estate, and get my cock inside of my wife.

I was her official, legal husband, now.

"Don't even think, for a moment, that we will have separate bedrooms," I laughed. "You will be staying in my chambers with me, wife," I told her.

She trembled in my hold, anticipation filling her as she grasped at my shoulders, pulling me into me and whispering out my name like a plea in gasping breaths as I kissed her more.

What a sexy, hot, wanton little thing...

When the train stopped, we made our way into a car that had arrived at the station to pick us up, and when that car stopped and butler Aaron opened the car door at the estate, he was startled to see me lift her into my arms and carry her out of the car as if the car were on fire, bursting forth from it and running.

I was keeping her in my arms all the way up the stairs and into the estate, through the manor to my chambers, before I tossed her on my bed.

I fell over top her, pulling the top of her outfit until the buttons popped off and the top burst open to expose her to my hungry gaze.

"You are my wife," I told her, hiking her skirt up and unbuttoning my pants, freeing myself.

I found my way into her body, her wet heat, as fast as I could manage while still turning her on and making sure she was wet for me.

She gasped, crying out and thrusting her hips up and into my own as she made thick, whining, wanton noises, *begging* for me.

I was all too happy to oblige her desires with my cock.

I hardened as I heard her breathy moans, her cries of my name like a mantra. I thrust into her with desperate slaps of our bodies coming together even as her squishy wet sounds filled the air.

I brought her to her peak, thrusting wildly again and again with my new addiction.

She took in all of my essence as I gave her all of myself, spending myself in her body, my release finding purchase to her waiting womb.

I wanted her...all of her.

I wanted to help her get her revenge on her parents, but most of all, I wanted her to belong to me just as I belonged to her.

I wanted to see her round with my sons and daughters. I wanted to see her give birth to our children.

I wanted to paint her entire body white with my cum while my cock slid in and out of her perfect, pristine, bright pink little pussy.

I couldn't possibly get enough of her.

Nivis's End, 1318 ILY

Just into the month, my twenty-first birthday arrived, and I became the duke.

My duchess was named at my side, and we stood, facing out to the crowd.

There were still many nay-sayers and whispers about my duchess, but she had already been titled, and there was no going back.

We hadn't done anything illegal. The only ones who had caused this were her parents, much to their own dismay, and I loved that it ate them alive.

I had heard, just days before, that Luther had overheard his parents fretting about what they were going to end up facing once Kathryn became the duchess.

As the ones who had pushed for her to marry my brother initially, they had essentially been the ones who brought her into this situation.

She was just taking her place as it were.

The blame was beginning to shift to them, now, and their reputation was falling. However, since Luther hadn't been involved, his family name and his worth as the marquess wasn't affected.

We were having the outcome that we had wished for, and we hadn't even done anything yet.

Solaris's Reign, 1318 SLY

It was Carson's third birthday, and we held a great birthday party for him, in his honor, to celebrate the occasion. I had food prepared for all of the underprivileged people of my fief, and the birthday party was open to all of the nobility.

Nobles of all titles came and brought gifts for the young marquess-to-be, and my duchess and I watched on with smiles and love in our hearts.

As it came time for the toast, my duchess surprised me when she stood, tapping her glass of...water...?

She usually enjoyed a glass of wine, or even champagne...

"It is with great pleasure that I thank you all for attending the birthday celebration of my young Carson Soren...and it is with just as much pleasure that I announce some big news...I am, *officially*, pregnant with the duke's child," she smiled at me, and I gaped at her.

It took a moment for the news to hit me fully, but I leapt up from my chair, taking her into my arms and bringing my lips to hers.

"How far?" I asked, overjoyed. "Are you serious?! I'm going to be a father? How far are you?!" I repeated the question, laughing.

She blushed. "About two months, your grace. Congratulations," she said, smiling at me and kissing me.

I laughed, taking her into my arms and spinning her in a gentle circle. "Oh, my! A baby. A father! A baby!" I laughed, overjoyed.

Everyone cheered, celebrating with us...save for *her* parents, who gaped in their usual horror.

"I have some news, as well," I said, motioning to the officers nearby.

I had not anticipated the announcement of my child, but I had known it was going to be a big event, so I had already made plans ahead of time. I had invited her parents, and requested for police officers.

I'd been sure to invite a detective and an officer— out of uniform, so that there wouldn't be any panic on the part of her parents.

It was the best opportunity that I would likely never get again...and it was already a joyous occasion.

"With the help of a detective and a private investigator, as well as *inside informants*...I have finally gained enough evidence to convict the former Marquess Abraham and his wife for the murder of my brother, Kenneth Soren, and setting the Soren estate on fire. There are witnesses, receipts of the assassin and the arsonist, and the check stub that they received on behalf of the insurance payment for my wife when the mansion was destroyed...that somehow, *she never actually received.*"

The entire crowd gaped and murmured, photos flashing as photographers took pictures of her parents in panic, crying out that they had been framed and fighting the officers as they filed into the room to seize them.

"It is with my sincerest hope that they never see the light of day again," Kathryn said, eyes hard.

"How could you do this?! How could you, when you're just the daughter of a *maid*!" The former Marchioness Abraham shouted.

"You dirty, filthy-bred brat! You illegitimate spawn!" Her father shouted. "I should have had the undertaker take you *along with* your mother!"

We froze, startled at the confession even as the marquess clamped a hand over his mouth.

"*What?*" I asked, startled.

I couldn't focus on anything else at that moment, though, when Kathryn fainted beside of me, and I caught her in my arms as the officers rushed her parents out of the estate.

"How is she?" The young Marquess Luther Abraham asked, clutching his own wife in his arms as they stood by my wife's bedside.

It had been three days since the party and the big revelation.

I shook my head. "It is hard to say. She had quite a shock. To find out that they murdered not only my brother—her former husband—but to also learn that they sent her *birth mother* off to be killed after giving birth?" I sighed. "It is a lot to process."

Luther nodded, sad. "I couldn't possibly ever make up for their misdeeds...but I would appreciate the opportunity to try," he said. "My poor sister...she was never really loved the way that I was. I always wanted to know why. I found out, when she married, why she'd been thrust into that marriage so quickly in the first place. But then, to learn the full truth...I feel so sorry for all of this."

"It isn't your fault, Luther," I said, patting his shoulder. "No one could have foreseen such a thing."

"Hmmm?" Kathryn finally stirred, and we startled, rushing to her side. I took her hand in my own.

"Kathryn?" I asked.

"K...Killian?" She asked, murmuring.

"Shh, darling, it is alright," I smiled at her as she looked at me. "Do not worry. Your parents have been sentenced to life in prison, and their names are utterly tarnished. Their titles stripped. The papers have reported everything truthfully, and in a surprising turn of events, the people are actually on your side. We have gotten our revenge and justice."

She smiled. "Thank you," she whispered, pulling me down to kiss her. "So...there's only one thing left that we need to discuss, then," she told me.

"Hm? And what is that, my love?" I smiled, stroking her hair.

"...Names. We need to discuss names," she said, serious, and I burst out a happy laugh even as her brother hugged her and we enjoyed filling her in on what she had missed.

She was so silly, but she was right.

I wanted to talk about the baby, and think about our futures together as a family.

"Yes, you are right. Let us discuss names."

Epilogue

Epilogue – Aaron Renaldas

Solaris's Gifts, 1320 Imperial Lunar Year

"Come on, now, Kenneth," Lord Killian coaxed the young master from young master Carson's grasp, and the child toddled toward him. "That's it, my boy!" He laughed, catching him as he stumbled. "Good effort, very good!"

I smiled peacefully, offering my duchess a glass of cold ice-tea, smiling as she stroked her swelling belly and watched her husband and sons.

Lord Carson was growing faster and faster, doing well in his tutoring and learning all the necessary skills he would need to become a good marquess one day. He was handsome and well-liked among the staff, and though he was being raised by Duke Killian, he did know him as "uncle," and referred to him as such.

Kenneth, named for his uncle's namesake, looked much like the duke himself. He had dark, shimmery brown hair, but his mother's bright, violet-shaded eyes. He was *just* over a year old, now, and was starting to walk more frequently. Carson loved to help him take his steps and teach him how to get around faster, ready for Kenneth to be running around with him.

Carson and Kenneth were thick as thieves, hardly separable.

This time around, the doctors told my duchess to expect a daughter, from what the mages' machines showed.

Duke Killian came and helped the duchess to stand, walking her back into the mansion as the maids motioned the boys along behind them.

"You don't have to coddle me," the duchess laughed.

"You shouldn't be in the heat for long periods, love," Killian insisted. "You are due anytime, now. I wouldn't want for you to strain yourself."

She laughed. "If this is a girl, hopefully you can shift your over-protective tendencies to her for a while and give me a break!" She giggled, and I smiled at them.

They had grown so close. Even closer than I had predicted, and I was so happy to see that my marchioness—now duchess—was finally happy. She was at peace in her life, with the man she loved and her own little family.

She had gotten her revenge on her parents for the deaths of Kenneth and her birth mother, and they were rotting in prison while Luther ruled over his marquessate and kept in close contact with my lady. He had his own family, now, and his children were coming over all the time to play with hers.

I knew, I just knew, that marquess Kenneth Soren was looking on with happiness for his brother and former wife.

Wouldn't you know it, only three days later, my duchess did give birth to a daughter.

A daughter with ashen-brown hair, like her mother, and bright, golden-green eyes like her father.

She was named Kennedy, another namesake for her uncle.

My duke and duchess lived quite happily for the rest of their days, and went on to have many grandchildren.

I was all too happy to watch over them, on behalf of my marquess, until my new marquess came of age to take over his title.

So ends the tale of this empathetic brother, who became a doting husband and father through a tragedy that turned out to be a blessing.

Bonus Chapter 1

Bonus Chapter 1 – Carson Soren...

Solaris's End, 1334 Imperial Lunar Year

"Please!" I heard a feminine voice cry as I was looking at some fruits at a stand in town. "Stop that thief!" She cried.

I whipped around, and saw a man holding a purple bag and bolting in my direction. A young woman, a teenager from the looks of it, was chasing after him desperately, hand reached out in an effort to grab him.

I stepped in his line of escape and pulled out my cane, swinging at just the right moment and catching his leg.

He flew through the air, crying out as he hit the ground and rolled—hard.

The officers that had been following behind her caught up and put him in handcuffs, and I picked up her bag. I brushed it off, and brought it to her.

"Are you alrig—" I started, but I froze when my eyes met hers.

Bright green eyes, light brown hair, beautiful tan skin...

She was stunning.

My heart immediately thumped hard in my chest.

"Thank you," she said, taking her bag from me and hugging it to her. "I only had one thing in here that I wanted to save, but the thief just wouldn't listen." She dug through, and pulled out a small, wrinkled photograph—a portrait of a woman who looked strikingly like her there.

"Is that—?"

"It is my mother. She...she died when I was young, and I barely remember her. This is all that I have of her, and I carry it with me everywhere. You saved my last remnants of her," she said, tearing up as she met my eyes. "Thank you so much," she told me.

I blushed, rubbing the back of my head. "My father died when I was a toddler, so I understand. All I have left of him is this," I said, showing her my father's watch. My step-father—and uncle—had passed it along to me as a gift when I had turned eighteen.

"Oh, I see," she said. "That is lovely," she said.

"She looked lovely, too, just like you," I said.

She blushed up at me.

"I'm Ellaine," she told me, holding her hand out to me.

"Carson," I said, taking her hand and squeezing.

We smiled at one another as my guards came and told me that the man was being arrested, and I invited her out to dinner that night.

We began courting a month later, and married six months after that, getting onto a train and heading off for our own estate to start our new lives together.

Two years later, we welcomed a beautiful set of twins—two boys who looked like their mother.

• • •
253

Another two years later, we would welcome a daughter who favored me, and one more year later, we would have one more son who looked like my father.

They grew up with a lot of cousins, and my mother was the best grandmother that I could have wished for my children to have.

Her father, who was still a single father, was a great man who loved our children.

He had not been titled, and society disagreed with a marquess marrying a commoner, but that didn't mean anything to me.

We had a good life, and a bright future ahead for our descendants.

It was a peaceful, blissful life.

—*Fin*—

Extra Content

Author's Medical Corner:

Believe it or not, a serious medical condition was referenced in this novel!

Many fire-related deaths actually have less to do with the flames, and more to do with the smoke.

In case of a fire, place a damp cloth over your mouth and nose if possible, and make sure to breathe through your nose as much as possible.

Here are some helpful tips and reference material!

Images News Videos Shoppin

People also ask

What are the odds of dying from smoke inhalation?

Do more people die from smoke inhalation than burns?

An estimated **50%-80% of fire deaths are the result of smoke inhalation injuries (rather than burns).** Oct 30, 2019

https://blog.coltinfo.co.uk › smoke-...

Smoke inhalation is the most important cause of fire ...

MORE RESULTS

| Images | News | Videos | Shoppin

People also ask

What are the odds of dying from smoke inhalation?

Do more people die from smoke inhalation than burns?

An estimated **50%-80% of fire deaths are the result of smoke inhalation injuries (rather than burns).** Oct 30, 2019

https://blog.coltinfo.co.uk › smoke-...

Smoke inhalation is the most important cause of fire ...

MORE RESULTS

| Images | Videos | Perspectives |

People also ask

What to do if you're trapped in a house fire?

If you must escape through smoke, **get low and go under the smoke to your exit**. Close doors behind you. If smoke, heat or flames block your exit routes, stay in the room with doors closed. Place a wet towel under the door and call the fire department or 9-1-1.

https://www.redcross.org › get-help
What To Do If A Fire Starts | American Red Cross

MORE RESULTS

| Images | Shopping | Videos | New

How do you put out fire on your skin?

Should you cover your mouth in a fire?

If there's smoke, crawl under the smoke and use a cloth, if possible, to cover your mouth and nose. Smoke and heat rise, so the air is clearer and cooler near the floor. If your escape route is blocked, shut the door immediately and use an alternate route, such as the window.

https://www.milpitas.gov › What-to...

What to do During a Fire | Milpitas, CA

MORE RESULTS

Images | Shopping | Videos | Nev

Why do you use a wet towel in a fire?

Protect your lungs: If it's still smoky in your room, breathe through a wet towel that covers your nose and mouth. Breathe only through your nose. Grip part of the towel with your lips and teeth. It can help remind you not to breathe through your mouth.

http://trip.ustia.org › safety › tips

What To Do If Trapped Inside Your Room During a Hotel Fire? - TRIP

MORE RESULTS

Extras:

Name pronunciations and illustrations:

Kathryn: Kah-thrihnn

Kenneth: Kih-nihth

Killian: Kih-lee-ehn

We hope you enjoyed The Royal's Saga,
Book 8:
The Empathetic Brother
Please join us for the next installment of The Royal's Saga: Book 9 –

The Anonymous Writer...

Coming soon! Scheduled for release on
November 29th, 2023!
Happy Thanksgiving and Happy Holidays!

Book Excerpt to follow

KRISTEN ELIZABETH

The ANONYMOUS Writer

2ND AND FINAL REVISION
EXTENDED AUTHOR'S ART EDITION

9

Book 9 Excerpt
Cadence Drake

Seed's Sewn, 1517 Imperial Lunar Year

"Another letter, my lady," the butler told me, bowing as he offered out a silver platter holding my letter.

Giddiness rushed through my heart as I took the letter, unfolding the envelope and reading the words.

"Dear mistress Drake,

It brings me great joy upon receiving your letters each time that they arrive.

I worry that I bore you in comparison to the elation that I feel upon getting your words, for you must have many men write to you.

I do wonder, how does a lady of your rank have any time for writing when you must have many pen-pals?

I wish that I could meet you, though I am afraid that my status would simply embarrass you, for you know well that I am not a great lord...I am but a knight.

However, if you would like to meet me as well, I would gladly ignore my status to have that chance.

Eagerly awaiting more words from you, my lady.

Signed, the longing knight,"

I smiled over the words of his letter, the letters of each word, the construction of the sentences...

He had wooed me for quite a while, and though I knew that he was a knight who had mistakenly received one of my letters one time and had been my pen-pal since...we had never decided to meet in person, and hadn't ever met to my knowledge.

I didn't even know which household he was a knight for.

As the daughter of an archduke, the niece of an emperor...I knew that an ordinary knight was below my station, and my father would never approve of marrying me off to someone of lower rank than a marquess. There were many noble families who had their sons to become knights, but my pen-pal had not once told me his father's rank...only that he was a knight for a noble house.

That could mean that he was hired by them and on a salary—which, granted, meant that he must be fairly skilled, to be hired by a noble family—or, that could mean that he was a noble and titled and was only a knight for honor's sake.

I was fifteen, now, and I knew that my marriage would be coming up soon. I had already been hearing of prospective husbands, since I was supposed to marry by the time that I turned eighteen...though, I wasn't sure how my father would find this challenge met.

Contrary to the knight's letter, I did not, in fact, have a lot of men writing to me. In fact, I was a social pariah, and was humiliated almost every time I stepped out of my home.

My father...hated me.

I was his only legitimate child, but...I was also his only daughter.

He made little secret—at least, in the privacy of our home—to how much he despised me.

Getting rid of me was both his most sought-after goal, but also the most elusive.

I would become engaged, if he had anything to do with it, when I turned sixteen at my debutante ball, and my chosen suitor—hand selected by my esteemed father—would be my escort to the ball.

I sighed, imagining a handsome knight by my side instead. That would surely be better than a high and mighty nobleman who would humiliate me and hate me the way that my father had my mother.

I would have an escort knight as well, of course, but he wouldn't be my actual partner.

I knew, vaguely, what my pen-pal looked like.

He had told me that he had light, ashen-grey hair, and walnut-colored eyes, but there were several knights even in my own household's knighthood who could fit this very description.

It was a fairly common hair and eye color in this region, so that was vague and didn't help me much.

I didn't know whose household he was even a knight for, though, and he told me that he didn't wish to tell me yet.

I sighed, grabbing the parchment, and writing out my reply.

"Dear Longing Knight,

    I would like to meet you, though I wonder if I already have. You tell me that you wish not to tell me to whose household you are a knight, but I keep trying to picture you in my mind's eye and I wonder if I have already seen your face and just not known.

    How I wish you could tell me...

    You seem to know me, and have even mentioned that you like my lustrous hair and my eyes, meaning that you have at least seen me...the suspense is antagonizing.

    I know not how much longer I will be able to write to you this way, as my father desperately seeks to sell me off in marriage as quickly as he possibly can. He would have already, if he could have.

    I am, sadly, the bearer of bad news to report to you that despite my rank...I am not as popular and desirable as you may imagine.

    I don't want to tell you that truth, but you would know if you saw me out in society. I am a target for harassment and humiliation.

    Oh, but please ignore my complaints. I realize, being born with a silver spoon in my mouth, I have no rights to make qualms about my status or my situation.

Rather, I should be grateful...but I wish not to marry a man who I barely know, who may treat me any way he wishes after we wed. I dream of romance, not an arrangement for father's benefit.

I would be greatly pleased to meet you, at least once, before I am to be married...or even before I am engaged, but I do not know if you can do this.

Wishing for more of your words, and asking you to call me by my first name...upon our first meeting,

Lady Cadence Elaine Drake."

I sealed the letter, and sent it off with the maid who waited by the door, who knew that I would be sending off a letter in response.

I hoped that my recent incentive—the beautiful ruby broach that I had given her that morning—was enough to make sure that she didn't tell anyone about my secret pen-pal.

My father would never allow me to write a knight this way.

I could only pray that he would honor my wish...and soon............
......
....
....
....
....
....
....
....
....

....Want to keep reading?

Be sure keep an eye out for the release of
The Royal's Saga, Book 9: The Anonymous Writer!

It only gets better from here, and let us not forget: STEAMIER.

...Y
U...
...M

Books by Kristen Elizabeth

>The Royal's Saga<

The Apathetic Knight, Part 1 – The Crowning
The Apathetic Knight, Part 2 – The Burning
The Apathetic Knight, Part 3 – The Freezing
The Villainous Princess, Part 1 – The Trapped
The Villainous Princess, Part 2 – The Freed
The Disregarded Dragon
The Hidden Queen
The Conquering Empress
The Abandoned Prince
The Decoy Duchess
>The Empathetic Brother<
The Anonymous Writer
The Luxurious Slave
The Incensed Guardian Novella
The Royal's Behind the Scenes Finale Novella

The Shifter's Saga

The Rejected Lady Book 1: Parts 1 & 2
The Rejected Lady Book 2: Parts 3 & 4

…Further titles coming soon!

The Lover's Saga

Titles coming soon!

The Spell-Caster's Saga

Titles coming soon!

The Dreamer's Saga

Titles coming soon!

The Queen's Saga

Titles coming soon!

The Knight's Saga

Titles coming soon!

The Immortal's Saga

Titles coming soon!

The Villain's Saga

Titles coming soon!

The Children's Saga (PG13)

Titles coming soon!

Acknowledgments

    A special thanks to my proof reader & good friend, Trisha, for reading through the novels and helping me with the grammatical and spelling aspects. Without your help, there were a lot of mistakes that would have made it into the books, and you encouraged me a ton. Thank you for your interest and investment in the story! I love you.

    A thanks to the Ghost-Writer who helped me with some editing, some of the ideas, and some of the bonus content added to the original story. You rock, and I appreciate that. Thank you so much!

    A special thanks to those who supported my work, including but not limited to, Sammie-Anne, Shannon, Amber, and so on. Several people who really encouraged me to write, publish and seek higher things. You guys inspired me to make this possible. I appreciate it so much. Special thanks goes to my most avid of fans, including Christine, Jeanna, and a few others who had been following my work and have gone to extra measures above and beyond to support and read my works.

    All of you aforementioned people make writing the books so much more exciting so that I can see your reactions and give you good books to read!

    Thank you all for being amazing. Without you, there is no way I would have gotten such a great start!

    A special thanks to my husband, Reece, for allowing me to take so much time to write and keeping everything running, and not complaining a ton.

You wanted me to pursue my goals, and I needed that extra push because I'm bad about procrastinating on things. I love you, handsome ;)

Lastly, I want to give a special thanks to my mom. You don't read my work or really think this will go that far, but you love me and try to support me the best you can. Thank you for everything, and I love you.

Thank you all so much <3

About the Author

Kristen Elizabeth is now on social media! Follow on Instagram and Tiktok! Handle for both apps is

lovelymadness92

She also has an author's page on Facebook! Check her out at

Kristen Elizabeth
(Lovely Madness Fantasies)

Follow for more bonus content, updates, and publishing schedules!

Kristen spent the majority of her life emersed in arts and music, and used writing and reading as an opportunity to escape from the trauma and depression that spiraled out of control from the background that she crawled out of.

Writing, arts and music opened up an entirely new world for her, and she kept herself surrounded by it to avoid the stress and anxiety that was forcing down on her.

Kristen, herself, is also on the Autism Spectrum, and wants to share her unique worlds with those around her.

She hopes someone out there will enjoy her creations as much as she does and use her creations to escape from the mundane everyday life.

Kristen's biggest goal is to fit somewhere outside of the norm, and to broaden horizons in the world of fiction.

Life isn't always happy endings, sunshine, and rainbows.

Sometimes, life is an utter freakshow and things don't work out the way you hoped.

That's something that Kristen wants to bring to her writing.

Let Kristen help you fall into her world of Lovely Madness ;)

None of this happens without the readers! Please help me by sharing and spreading the word means so much to me!

Thank you so much!

I hope you tune in for Book 9:
The Anonymous Writer!

Author Q&A

Q: Where do you get the ideas?

A: I am autistic, so my brain is almost constantly running at warp-speeds with ideas. I have over one-hundred novel ideas right now, currently, and over seventy started.

Q: What is your writing process like?

A: My process is simple—I get a new notebook, and begin writing down basic ideas in the beginning. Once I have an idea I like and that I would like to expand on, I begin the process of "storm-boarding." This is where I lay out my main Female Lead, Male Lead, trope ideas, general ideas, an antagonist or issue, and how they get past it. Then, I lay out charts of family trees, timelines, tie in histories...it can be a length process, and that is what takes the longest.

Q: What is the fastest you have typed up a novel?

A: A week. With every book, I write the first three chapters before I move on to the next story, and write the first three chapters...that way, when I go back to finish the story, I simply re-read what I have so far, and I just let it flow out of me. I don't usually read over it or check it until I am going through for editing purposes. I do, however, keep my basic storm-boards in mind and try to keep things as close to the written layout and ideas as possible, without deviating.

Q: How many books did you publish the first/first and second editions for?

A: Books 1.0, 1.5, 2, 3, 4, 5, 6, 7, and 8...so, total, 9 books published. I stopped publishing to revise the books and create the special Author's Art Edition of the saga.

Q: How many books are in this saga?

A: 13 novels, and 2 novellas.

Q: Will all of your novels tie in together the way that 1.0 and 1.5 are?

A: That is my intention, currently. In this saga, it will mention other characters from the saga in each book, but years do pass between the settings of each book, so it isn't quite a, "I'm the Female lead, meeting the Female lead of this novel."

About this Book

The Empathetic Brother, firstly of all, is a self-publication made possible by Amazon Self-Publishing KDP.

The author spent close to a year putting together this novel. The original drafts and stormboards were crafted in five-subject notebooks, before being made into manuscripts.

Most of my typing is done between 8pm and 12am, as my children are the light of my life and I do not take time away from them to work. (When they are in school, of course it is a different matter, though, and I have normal working hours until they get home.) Overall, typing up the story took about six months.

This work is entirely fiction, and is entirely original material from the author.

The original 1st edition of—

"The Royal's Saga, Book 8: The Empathetic Brother was published on June 10th, 2023.

It had roses as the cover.

The original book 230 pages long!

Finally, last but not least, this new edition of The Empathetic Brother – Author's Art Edition is the final release of the self-published version of the novel, there are tons of added dialogue and author's hand-drawn art featured!

No other release of this novel will take place unless it is brought into a publishing house and released with tons of new features.

Thank you again to all of you readers!

You are amazing, and I hope you enjoy the rest of the novel series!

Please review the story, and please share with friends! One of my biggest dreams is to see people unboxing my story and enjoying the worlds that I take them to within it.

Much Lovely Madness to you all!

#TheRoyalsSaga

#TheEmpatheticBrother

#SteamyRomance

#KristenElizabeth

#LovelyMadnessFantasies

Kristen Elizabeth
Letting you fall into a
world of
Lovely Madness

Reader's Observing Questions:

Q: Who was your favorite character? Why?

Q: What do you think will happen in Book 9, The Anonymous Writer?

Q: How did this book make you feel?

Q: Were you surprised by the ending of this novel and how the story turned out?

Q: Were there any predictions you made about this book that did come true?

Q: What did you think the novel would be like, based on the cover and preview in Book 7?

Q: Do you want to read Book 9? Because it will be released soon!

I hope you enjoyed the book! I hope you keep following the journey that this story takes!

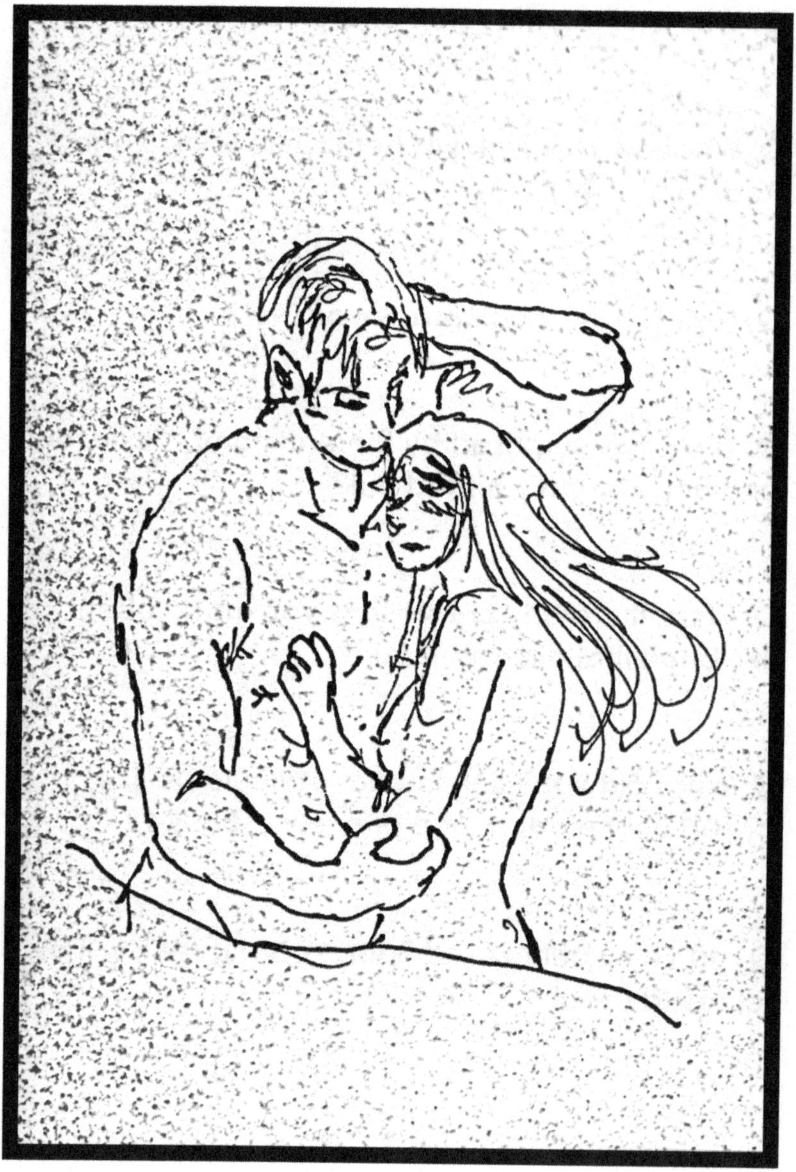

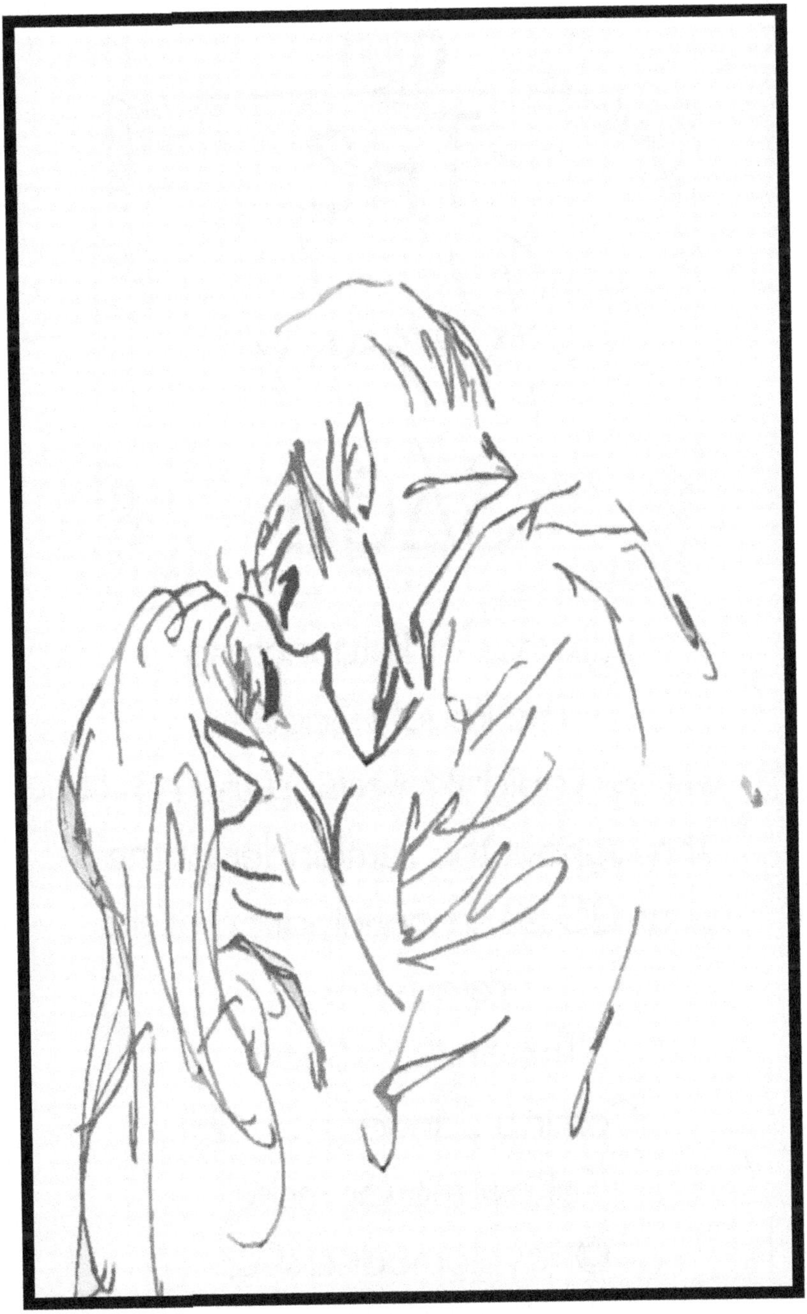

KRISTEN ELIZABETH

THE Royal's SAGA

In honor of Relaunching
The Royal's Saga,
I will be Rapid-Realeasing the novels
throughout the remainder of the
year 2023, in anticipation of the
release of
The Shifter's Saga
Coming January, 2024!
Follow me for more!
@ lovelymadness92
Insta & tiktok!

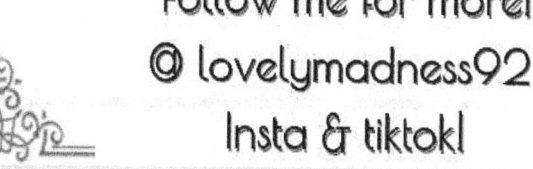

Lovely Madness Fantasies

Kristen Elizabeth

FANTASY ROMANCE AUTHOR

Final Remarks

Thank you so much for reading
Kristen Elizabeth's novel world of
Lovely Madness

The Royal's Saga, Book 8:
The Empathetic Brother
2nd Edition; "Author's Art Edition."

Made in the USA
Columbia, SC
27 May 2024